Michael Pearce was raised in Anglo-Egyptian Sudan, where his fascination for language began. He later trained as a Russian interpreter but moved away from languages to pursue an academic career, first as a lecturer in English and the History of Ideas, and then as an administrator. Michael Pearce now lives in South-West London and is best known as the author of the award-winning *Mamur Zapt* books.

A Dead Man in Barcelona

Michael Pearce

Constable • London

CONSTABLE

First published in Great Britain in 2008 by Constable,
an imprint of Constable & Robinson Ltd.

This paperback edition published in 2017 by Constable

1 3 5 7 9 10 8 6 4 2

A CIP catalogue record for this book
is available from the British Library.

ISBN: 978-1-47212-609-2

Typeset in Palatino by Photoprint, Torquay
Printed and bound in Great Britain by
CPI Group (UK), Croydon CR0 4YY

Papers used by Constable are from well-managed forests and other
responsible sources.

MIX
Paper from
responsible sources
FSC® C104740

Constable
An imprint of
Little, Brown Book Group
Carmelite House
50 Victoria Embankment
London EC4Y 0DZ

An Hachette UK Company
www.hachette.co.uk

www.littlebrown.co.uk

Chapter One

'The coffins came out of the church . . .'

'Yes?'

'And the men put them down on the ground . . .'

'Yes?'

'And then – then the lids opened and the bodies got out.'

There was a short silence.

'Got out?'

'That's right.'

'The bodies?'

'Yes. There were three of them. Look, I know it's hard to believe –'

'It certainly is,' said the Deputy Commissioner.

'It gave me a shock, I can tell you.'

'Well, it would. I can see that.'

'You obviously don't believe me,' said Hattersley.

'No, no, of course I believe you,' said the Deputy Commissioner heartily, looking at the clock.

'One of them was a young woman.'

Yes, thought Seymour, sex probably went with it, poor chap.

The Deputy Commissioner looked at him sharply and frowned. Surely he had not said that out loud?

'Three of them, did you say?' he said hastily, hoping to cover up.

'Yes. Of course, they weren't really dead.'

'No, no. Of course. No, they wouldn't be.'

'I spoke to one of them. The young woman. And she said it was to remember those fallen in Semana Tragica.'

'Semana Tragica?' said Seymour, waking up. 'Tragic Week?'

'Yes. That's why I thought . . .' Hattersley looked at the man from the Foreign Office who had brought him but, receiving no encouragement, his voice tailed away.

Then he continued determinedly however.

'And then she said, "You're English, aren't you?" "From Gibraltar," I said. "Ah, then you'll have known Sam Lockhart?" "I know Sam Lockhart, yes." "And do you know how he died?" she said. "Yes. No, that is, at least, not exactly."

'"Well, you ought to find out," she said. "Tell your English friends that. Tell the English people." And then she went back into the church.'

Hattersley looked round the table.

'Well, that's it,' he said. 'That's all. But I thought –'

'You did quite right to tell us,' said the man from the Foreign Office. 'Thank you, Mr Hattersley.'

'A nut,' said the Deputy Commissioner.

'Yes. Quite possibly,' said the man from the Foreign Office. 'But –'

'You are surely not expecting us to take an interest?' said the Deputy Commissioner.

'Well –'

'Someone ought to,' said a man who had not yet spoken. Seymour had somehow formed the impression that he was an Admiral.

'But not, I think, us,' said the Deputy Commissioner. 'The Foreign Office, perhaps?'

'Of course we *have* taken an interest. From the first. Naturally, since he was an Englishman.'

'What's all this about Gibraltar?'

'He came from Gibraltar.'

'In that case, I think it's all the more a question for the Foreign Office. I mean, he's hardly even English!'

'Hold on, hold on!' said the man from the Foreign Office hastily. 'That is, actually, one of the points in dispute. We say he is, the Spanish say he's not.'

'Surely that can easily be established?'

'Easily be established?' said the man from the Foreign Office, reeling back. 'We have been arguing about it with Spain for over two hundred years!'

'Hmm, yes, I see,' said the Deputy Commissioner. 'Nevertheless, I still feel it is something for you to address rather than for Scotland Yard.'

'Of course, we *have* been addressing it.'

'For two years,' snorted the man whom Seymour took to be an Admiral.

'Well, it takes time,' protested the man from the Foreign Office. 'One has to go through the right channels and they are not always responsive.'

'They wouldn't be, would they?' said the man whom Seymour took to be an Admiral. 'Since he was in their hands when he died.'

'In their –?'

'He was in prison when he died,' said the man from the Foreign Office.

'In prison?' said the Deputy Commissioner incredulously. 'You mean ... No, really, this doesn't sound at all like the thing for us. A foreign national? Or the next best thing to a foreign national. In a foreign country.'

'Just a minute!' said the Admiral.

'And now you tell me he was actually in prison when he died? No, really,' the Deputy Commissioner said, shaking his head, 'this really is not the thing for us.'

'The Prime Minister doesn't think so,' murmured the man from the Foreign Office.

'Prime Minister?' said the Deputy Commissioner, taken aback. 'What the hell does he know about it?'

'Nothing,' said the Admiral. 'But he knows about *us*.'

'Us?'

'The Navy.'

'Well, I'm sure. But –'

'Gibraltar,' said the Admiral, as to an idiot. '*Ships. Docks.*'

'Oh, yes, I see. And the Navy is taking an interest –'

'It certainly is.'

'Well, of course, that puts a different complexion on it.'

'I should hope so.'

'But,' said the Deputy Commissioner, 'I'm afraid I still don't see why Scotland Yard –'

'We feel,' said the man from the Foreign Office, 'that the thing calls for professional investigation.'

'We certainly do,' said the Admiral.

'So naturally we turn to –'

'Yes,' said the Deputy Commissioner glumly. 'Yes. But –'

'And so does the Prime Minister.'

'And the Navy,' said the Admiral.

'Yes, well –' said the Deputy Commissioner, depressed.

'Of course,' said the man from the Foreign Office cunningly, 'Scotland Yard need not be formally involved.'

'Needn't it?' said the Deputy Commissioner, brightening.

'In fact, it might be best if it's not.'

'Well, there is that,' said the Deputy Commissioner, brightening still further.

'All that's needed is a man. And he could be seconded.'

'To the Foreign Office?' said the Deputy Commissioner hopefully.

'Oh, no. No, I don't think so. That would *not* be appropriate. To the Navy.'

'What?' said the Admiral.

'You're always having stores pinched, aren't you?'

'Well, I wouldn't quite say –'

'We could put it out that you've asked for a man from Scotland Yard to be assigned to help you with the inquiries you are no doubt making.'

There was a pause.

And then, unexpectedly, the Admiral gave a great laugh.

'That'll put the fear of God into a few people!' he said.

'Well, then! And I think we've got just the right man, haven't we? Mr Seymour has worked with us before and we have every confidence in his ability to handle things discreetly. And he speaks Spanish.'

'And he knows about docks,' said the Deputy Commissioner.

'Do you?' said the Admiral eagerly, turning to Seymour.

'English ones,' said Seymour hastily. 'And dockland rather than docks. I normally work in the East End.'

'At least you've bloody heard of them,' said the Admiral.

'What the hell is Tragic Week?' said the Deputy Commissioner, as they walked down the stairs.

'It happened two years ago,' said Seymour. 'The Spanish Government called up reserves to fight in Spanish Morocco. The reserves were conscripts, mostly from Catalonia, the bit of Spain that Barcelona is in. When they were ordered on to the ships, they refused to go, and most of Catalonia supported them. There were riots in the streets and the Army was called in to put them down. Which it did. Bloodily.'

'And this man Lockhart was mixed up in it?'

'Apparently.'

'It sounds even less our kind of thing,' said the Deputy Commissioner. 'In fact, it doesn't sound our kind of thing at all.'

That was Seymour's private opinion, too. When the Deputy Commissioner had called him in, however, he had jumped at the chance. This was because he had his own reason for going to Spain: and her name was Chantale.

Chantale did not come from Spain, actually, but from Morocco, and French Morocco, not Spanish, at that. But the two were next door to each other and both were just across the Straits and it would surely be possible for him to slip across at some point in the assignment?

And he needed to slip across, for there were things to be resolved. Chantale was half Arab, half French. This had been awkward for her in Morocco because she had been neither fish nor fowl. The French had eyed her askance, conscious all the time of what some of them referred to as the touch of the tar-brush. The Arabs had mistrusted her because they had never known to which side she would fall when the chips were down. Chantale herself had not been sure, either; which was why she had been tempted by Seymour's argument, at the end of a previous mission in Tangier, that the thing to do was put both sides behind her and become something else: British, for instance. With him.

Tempted, but there had been other things to consider. Her mother, for instance; definitely Arab and definitely Moroccan. Could she be abandoned? Her mother, strong-willed, had said yes. Chantale was not so sure. And then, what about all that emotional investment she had made in the Nationalist hopes she had had for a new, young country independent of foreign domination? Or was that all a waste of time, anyway, now that the French had taken over and should she make the safer investment with the people currently on top, the French occupying power? All this had been precipitated a year ago when Seymour had been sent to Morocco on an assignment; and she was still dangling.

Seymour was dangling, too. He wanted, more than anything in the world, he told himself, to be with her. But with her in London's grimy East End? Where the sun she was used to never penetrated through the pea-soup fog? Where you never quite shook off the chill of the docks? Was it fair to ask her?

Never mind the fairness, he had come to the conclusion; just ask her. But, in a way, he had not been sorry at her uncertainty. It reflected his own.

So they had both jumped at the chance when he had been given the assignment in Spain. It was neutral ground and maybe that would help them to sort things out. For Seymour, who always thought the glass was half full, it was well on the way to England. For Chantale, in whose experience the glass was nearly always half empty, it was a tentative step from which she could easily retreat.

The looseness of the assignment favoured them. It would give Seymour a chance to compose his own programme; and surely that programme could be tweaked to enable him to slip across the Straits to see her?

At the last moment, though, it had been Chantale who had decided to slip; and she would be arriving the day after Seymour.

And what he was thinking now, as he waited at the bottom end, the docks end, of Las Ramblas, Barcelona's great, humming, tree-lined boulevard, was that Chantale would feel at home here. This part of Barcelona, the part nearest the docks, was like an Arab town. There were Arabs in long galabeahs lounging at street corners, women in dark veils and burkas keeping to the walls as they walked down the street with their baskets. In the open doorways of the houses men were sitting smoking bubble pipes, the bowls bubbling on the ground beside them. Further along the street was a little market and at the stalls, loaded with giant tomatoes, bursting peppers and bulging aubergines, he could hear people speaking, and what they were speaking was not Spanish but Arabic.

In front of him was a small church, the church Hattersley had spoken about. It had white walls, dazzlingly white in the bright sunshine, but blackened doors. He went across to it and looked in.

And reeled back. The porch was full of arms and legs!

Arms and legs? He looked again and saw now that they were plaster, like the two statues standing beside the door.

11

And there were also plaster casts, used surgical ones, neatly cut off and obviously taken from people's limbs when they had served their purpose. Some had come from children and had little pictures drawn on them.

He realized now what they were. They were votive offerings, thanksgivings for injuries received and now cured. He had seen some once in a Catholic church in the East End. They had seemed to him at first grotesque but then rather moving.

In among the casts were stained bandages. Bloodstained bandages. He was looking at them when a voice beside him said:

'Semana Tragica. The Tragic Week.'

It was an elderly man.

'Tragic Week?' said Seymour. 'But that was – well, two years ago.'

'The memories are still here,' the man said. 'Although sometimes not the people.'

'Not the people, no.'

'You are, perhaps, remembering someone?'

'No. At least – well, yes, I suppose. There was an Englishman. His name was Lockhart.'

The elderly man looked at him sharply.

'I knew Lockhart,' he said. 'But he didn't die here.'

'No. He died in prison.'

'You know this, then?'

'Yes. But not much more. I would like to know more.'

The man was silent. He seemed to be thinking. Then he made up his mind.

'A coffee, perhaps!'

There was a café nearby and they went in. The man ordered two coffees but then didn't seem in any hurry to begin. He looked at Seymour once or twice as if considering.

'You speak Spanish well,' he said, 'but you are not Spanish.'

'I'm British.'

'Ah, British. Like Lockhart.'

'That's right.'

The man nodded, as if satisfied.

'It is as well to establish these things,' he said, 'before you talk. They are always sending round informers.'

He looked round the café.

'We shall be all right here,' he said. 'This is a Catalan café.'

And now Seymour understood. He had been listening with half an ear to the conversation in the café and had been puzzled. More than puzzled: disconcerted. He had thought he understood Spanish pretty well, but he had found it oddly difficult to follow the conversation in the café. It seemed Spanish and it was easy to make out the sense of it. But it was not Spanish. There were different words and different inflexions.

'Ah!' he said. 'I've got it. Catalan is new to me. But I can see now –'

The man put his hand on Seymour's arm.

'One moment, Señor. I will let them know you're English.'

He went over to the counter and said something to the man at the till.

Then he came back.

'It's all right now,' he said. 'They can relax.'

He sipped his coffee and put the cup down.

'You speak Spanish very well,' he said, 'but Spanish is not the thing to speak here.'

Seymour nodded.

'Thank you for telling them,' he said. 'And for telling me.'

He sipped his coffee.

'There are people here who knew Lockhart.'

'Can I talk to them?'

'You had better talk to Dolores.'

He signalled with his hand and a waitress came over.

'Dolores, this is a friend of mine. He would like to talk to you.'

'Señor?'

'I am an Englishman and I would like to talk to you about an Englishman. His name is Lockhart.'

'I knew Lockhart,' she said.

'Well?'

'Too well. He was my husband.'

'Dolores!' said the elderly man reprovingly.

'Well, almost. That's what he used to say. As good as. He always used to stay with me when he came to Barcelona. And he used to say that one day he would take me back with him.'

'To Gibraltar?'

'That's right.'

'Dolores,' protested the elderly man, 'he had a wife already.'

'I know, but there would have been room for another. I wouldn't have made any fuss. We could have managed.'

'Dolores, he was spinning you along.'

'Don't all men do that?' She shrugged. 'Anyway, I didn't mind. It was nice to think of him in that way. That's the way he thought of me, too. As his wife. Almost.'

'He was staying with Dolores that night,' said the elderly man.

'When –?'

'When it happened,' said the elderly man, pulling up a chair for her to sit down. 'Tell him.'

'We heard shooting,' she said. 'There had been trouble. Those boys. They were making them go on the ships. There had been shooting before but this time it was close, just outside, in the street. "This is the stuff!" he said. He was quite excited. And then he wanted to go out. "You'd do better to stay in," I said. "You don't want to get mixed up in this. You stick to business." "Ah, but this *is* business," he said.'

'What did he mean by that?'

'I don't know. I didn't know what he was talking about.'

'What was his business?'

'Something to do with the docks. He had an office down there. Just past the church. But I never quite knew what his business was. We didn't talk about it. Well, you wouldn't, would you? In bed? Anyway, that night he insisted on going out. And then he didn't come back.

'There was more shooting, not just in our street but in all the streets, and I got frightened and ran back here to the café. And Manuel – he's the boss, he owns the café – said, "You stay right here until it's all over." He said that to all of us, and we all stayed. "There's no point in getting mixed up in it," he said. "It's not your fight."

'But Inez – she's another of the waitresses – said it was her fight. She's Catalan, you see. Well, I am, too, but not like her. I mean I wasn't sure it *was* my fight. But she said it was our boys, and she went out. And *she* didn't come back, either.

'I was in a hell of a state, I can tell you. We were all in a state. But Manuel said, "Just stay here. You'll be all right here." Although it didn't seem so.

'It was hours before the shooting stopped. But then Manuel went out. There were a lot of bodies, he said, but hers wasn't among them. He came back and said we should stay inside.

'But I wanted to see. I mean, he had looked for Inez but I wanted to look for Lockhart. So I went out and another of the girls came with me. But I couldn't find anything. He wasn't among the bodies. "That's good," Marie said. "It means he's alive." But I couldn't believe that. Not until I'd really seen him. They said a lot of people had been taken to the prison so I went along and asked to see him. But they wouldn't let me, they wouldn't let anybody. And then Manuel said to come home and he would fix it when things had settled down. So I went back to the café.

'And a couple of days later he did fix it and I went to see him.'

'You saw Lockhart when he was in prison?' said Seymour.

'Yes. I couldn't see him really properly, though, it was so dark. He was lying in a corner and I thought maybe he had been wounded, but he said not. He told me to go away and not come again. "Don't get mixed up in this!" he said. I said I could bring him things, food, perhaps. I wasn't sure that they'd fed him and I'm damned sure they weren't giving him enough water, but he said keep out of it. "Don't come back," he said. But I would have gone back. But then we heard that he was dead. Those bastards had killed him – killed him in the prison!'

Her voice had risen. Everyone else in the café had stopped talking. Then a man's voice said soothingly, 'It's okay, Dolores, it's okay. You come here now. Get back into the kitchen.'

Dolores got up from the table.

'I'd better go,' she said. She managed a smile. 'Or Manuel will have my ass.'

'Did he say anything else?'

'Only to tell Nina.'

'Who's Nina?'

'She's a girl in Barcelona. He always used to go and see her when he was over here. Why, I can't think, because she's a real pain in the ass. I used to wonder if he had a thing for her but I reckon not. It wouldn't be easy to get a thing going with Nina. It would be like being in bed with a hedgehog.'

'Did he say why?'

'No. Just told me to tell her. Well, I did, but that was a waste of time. She knew anyway. She just looked at me with those cold eyes and nodded. That was all. A hard bitch. As well as prickly.'

She set off across the room.

'I've got to go,' she said.

She was back, however, after two steps.

'Why do you want to know about Lockhart?' she demanded.

'Friends are interested in what happened to him,' he said. 'Friends in England,' he added with emphasis.

'Tell them to go on being interested,' she said fiercely. 'Tell them to ask questions and go on asking questions. In the end someone's got to answer.'

The conversation in the café resumed.

'You see?' said the elderly man. 'You see now how it was?'

'I am sorry,' said Seymour. 'I did not mean to upset her.'

The man shrugged.

'She'll get over it,' he said. 'It may even help her.'

He got up from the table and put out his hand.

'Marques,' he said. 'Ricardo Marques.'

'Seymour.'

'Do what she says: go on asking questions. Perhaps we will be able to help you.'

He shook Seymour's hand once more.

'We shall meet again,' he said.

An hour later Seymour was walking up Las Ramblas with Chantale. As it left the port area the street opened up and became an airy boulevard crowded with people. They seemed in no particular hurry, stopping frequently to chat with acquaintances or study the great bunches of flowers hung above the flower stalls. There were flowers everywhere, not just on the stalls but spread out in swathes of colour along the side of the road and bunched in miniature fields at the foot of the trees: roses, sweetpeas, carnations, chrysanthemums and great streaked tiger lilies whose powerful scent reached out right across the boulevard.

Everywhere, too, there seemed to be street performers, fire-eaters, jugglers, acrobats, dancers, and strange figures straight from a carnival, huge figures sometimes on stilts with grotesquely large papier-mâché heads. A Spanish word came into his mind: *cabezudos*. That's what they must be, *cabezudos*, the bizarre, capering figures that were part of every procession at carnival time.

The whole street was like a carnival. There were floats, there were musicians, there were clowns. From the floats people in bright costumes were throwing sweets for the children. The children dashed in among the *cabezudos* to retrieve the sweets and the *cabezudos* affected to trip over them. Everyone was laughing. Surely this must actually be a carnival? But no. He learned later that every day was like that on Las Ramblas.

Chantale, responding to the mood, had unbound the headscarf she normally wore in Tangier, even when she was in European dress, and let her hair fall down on to her shoulders.

If she had done that in Morocco it would have caused a riot. For some reason a woman's hair seemed especially sexually inflammatory to Arabs.

But here, on Las Ramblas, Chantale suddenly felt a great expansion of personal freedom, as if a huge weight had been lifted from her shoulders. She let her hair fall and felt as if she had come out into the sunshine.

Seymour had been recommended a hotel in a small square off Las Ramblas. The square was little more than a patch of baked mud surrounded by apartment blocks. The blocks were three or four storeys high and many had rooms with little balconies fenced in by a kind of iron fretwork. Children played on the balconies and from time to time women dressed in black would come out and pick one up. Then they would lean on the balcony and monitor events in the plaza below. There was a play area in one corner of the plaza and perhaps they were keeping an eye on other offspring.

Seymour suspected that a good deal of monitoring went on in the square. He knew that his arrival in the square earlier that day had been noticed and now Chantale's arrival with him was registered too. When he had asked for a room he had wondered whether to make it a double room but the suspicious eye of the proprietor suggested that it might be unwise. She was one of the landladies, he felt sure, who could tell at once whether a woman was married or unmarried: and he sensed that even in Barcelona that could still make a difference. In the end he had booked a separate room for Chantale.

After she had checked in they returned to Las Ramblas. There seemed to be more people there even than before. It was growing dark and the lamps had been lit. The street entertainers were out in force, often performing around braziers where they could be seen better.

In one place there were several braziers together and a space had been cleared where gypsy-like figures were dancing the flamenco. There was the click of castanets and someone was tapping on a small drum.

Cabezudos were stalking round the edges of the cleared space chatting to the spectators in Catalan.

'Does that *cabezudo* know you?' asked Chantale.

'No.'

'Well, it seems to be wanting to speak to you.'

'It can't be.'

The *cabezudo*, which was about eight feet tall, loomed over him.

'Señor, Señor!'

'*Si?*'

'Lockhart,' it said quietly, and then capered away.

He followed it to the edge of the crowd.

'You want to know about Lockhart?' it said in a hoarse whisper.

'I do; but how did you know that?'

'Ricardo told me.'

'Ricardo Marques?'

'*Si.*'

Seymour nodded. 'You're right, I do.'

'Talk to Nina.'

'Who is Nina?'

'A teacher. She teaches at the school in your square.'

19

Your square? He had moved into the hotel only the day before. How did they know about him?

'Just a minute!' he said.

But the *cabezudo* had danced away into the crowd, the huge head jerking comically as it chatted to people, throwing a gigantic, grotesque shadow as it emerged for a moment into the light of the braziers.

Chapter Two

'Nationalists?' said the Chief of Police, looking at him blankly. 'There are no Nationalists in Spain. Catalonian or otherwise.'

Seymour had gone to the police station early the next morning to present his credentials.

'But, surely, what happened in Tragic Week –'

'Tragic Week? Ah, terrible, terrible! But that was nothing to do with the Nationalists.'

'No?'

'No. Riff-raff. Criminals. Arabs. Anarchists. But –' The Chief of Police shook his head. 'Nationalists, no.'

'But I thought –'

'The Señor has been misinformed.'

The Chief of Police relented slightly.

'Of course, it's easy to get a wrong picture,' he said. 'The situation was very confused. I was confused myself. It all happened so suddenly! There was I, having breakfast on the patio, when the phone rings and my wife comes rushing out. "Alonzo," she said, "you'd better get off your ass. Things are happening."

'And then I heard it: shooting. "What the hell's that?" I said.

'"It's down by the docks," she said. "Those filthy Arabs again." (We've got a lot of Arabs in the docks, you see, Señor.) "Oh, is it?" I said. "I'll soon sort them out." And I went back into the bedroom to get my gun.

'And while I was there, there was a knock on the door,

and it was Pedro, one of my inspectors. "Chief," he said, "you'd better come. There's trouble down at the docks." "It's those bloody Arabs again, is it?" I said. "No, Chief, I don't think it is this time," he said. "It's more general. All hell is breaking loose."

'And when I got there, Christ, all hell *was* breaking loose! There was fighting everywhere. Shooting, burning, stones flying – stones flying everywhere! It was bloody mayhem. And after a bit of this I thought, this is not for us. You need the bloody Army. So I pulled my people out. And then I thought I'd better ring my bosses.

'But you can do that from home as well as from the office, can't you? And I felt in need of a drink. So I went home. And after a bit my wife said, "Come on, Alonzo, you've got to do something." "Why?" I said. "Because if you don't, Madrid will be on to you." And, Christ, the next minute there *was* Madrid on to me. "What's going on, Alonzo?" they said. "It's bloody war," I said. "There's fighting, there's shooting. The docks are in flames."

'"What are you doing about it?" they said. "Hadn't you better get stuck in?" "I did get stuck in," I said. "But I had to pull out. We were taking casualties. There are bloody hundreds of them. This isn't a thing for the police," I said. "It's something for the Army."

'Well, they went quiet at that. And then they said, "All right, Alonzo, we'll talk to Colonel Ramirez. And when you hear the Army's guns, you go down there and pick up the pieces."

'Well, we waited until we heard the Army's guns and then I said, "Right, we'd better get down there." But my wife tapped me on the shoulder and said, "Don't be in too much of a hurry to get down there, Alonzo. Wait until the Army's guns have stopped." She's got her head screwed on, my wife.

'And it was as well we didn't get down there too quickly, for the fighting went on for days. The best part of a week. But eventually the shooting stopped and I sent my lads in.

'"Pick them up!" I said. "Don't ask questions. Just bang them in. We can sort out the sheep from the goats later." So that's what we did. Picked up everyone in sight. Including, as it turned out, Señor Lockhart.'

'Including Señor Lockhart?'

The Chief of Police poured himself some water from a carafe standing on his desk, looked at the glass, a little disappointedly, it must be said, as if he had hoped that somehow the water had miraculously turned into wine, and sipped it. He put the glass down.

'Including Señor Lockhart,' he said. 'You have to understand, Señor, that all was confusion. We had no time to get life histories. We just took everybody in, no matter what they were doing. And if you think about it, Señor Seymour, that is not so unreasonable. If bullets are flying all over the place, you're not going to be just standing there, if you're nothing to do with it.'

'Bullets were still flying?' said Seymour. 'I thought you said you'd waited until –'

'The occasional bullet was still flying. *Enough* bullets were flying,' said the Chief of Police, wiping his mouth, 'to make honest people want to keep out of the way.'

'And that's when you arrested Señor Lockhart?'

'That's right.'

'What was he doing there?'

'That,' said the Chief of Police, 'is a good question.'

'But haven't you been able to answer it? Surely you've had enough time. All this happened two years ago!'

'It is rather more complicated than that,' said the Chief of Police. 'To start with, normally we would take statements as soon as a person was admitted. But we took so many people in that week that we couldn't. We were still working through them when we heard, alas, that Señor Lockhart had died.'

'Yes,' said Seymour, 'I am coming to that.'

'I thought you might be.'

'But even if Señor Lockhart died – especially since he died – surely an investigation was made?'

'Oh, yes. Of course. And a report is being drawn up.'

'*Is* being drawn up?'

'The investigation has not yet been completed.'

`After two years?'

The Chief of Police was silent for a moment. Then he said, 'Are you sure you *want* the investigation to be completed?'

'Want it?' said Seymour, taken aback. 'Of course we want it!'

'But are you sure? Even if it revealed something that perhaps was better not revealed?'

'Surely in circumstances like this, an inquiry *has* to be made. And if it is embarked on, it has to be completed.'

'And then?' said the Chief of Police.

'Well, what happens next depends on the circumstances. There will be several possibilities. A decision will have to be made by the appropriate authority.'

'And you think that procedure has not been followed?'

'I don't *know* that it's been followed. That's the point.'

'You don't think the authority may have some discretion in this? Over the publishing of the findings?'

'Well, in principle –'

'And may have exercised that discretion?'

'What are you saying? That there is some reason for hushing it up?'

The Chief of Police held up a hand. 'That there *may* be a reason. That discretion *may* have been exercised. There doesn't have to be anything sinister here. The reason may simply be in order not to distress the family unduly. Or there may be some wider reason. That it might distress a Government, say. Or complicate an already complicated situation.'

'You are saying this was the case here?'

'No. Just that it *may* be the case. We keep coming back, you see, to that question you asked, a very good

24

question. What exactly *was* Señor Lockhart doing during Tragic Week?'

'Was he taking sides, you mean?'

'Or did he have his own agenda? In which case, what exactly was that agenda? You see, Señor, even after all this time, these questions still have to be answered.'

'There is another question which has to be asked,' said Seymour. 'Even after all this time.'

'I know, I know!' said the Chief of Police.

'It is about how Lockhart came to die.'

'A shock!' said the Chief of Police. 'It came as a terrible shock. I couldn't believe it! I went home and told my wife and she couldn't believe it, either. A man like Señor Lockhart, known to all, respected by all. But in the midst of life we are in death, Señor Seymour. One moment Señor Lockhart was with us and the next he was taken away.

'"Let it be a warning to you, Alonzo," my wife said. "You, too, could be carried off if you go on the way you do. Remember, God has his eye on you!"

'"Father Roberto has his eye on me, more like, and has been talking again," I said.

'Don't get me wrong, Señor, my wife is a good woman and on the whole has her head screwed on all the way. But, between you and me, Señor, she listens a bit too much to the people in black. She's always there at the church, morning, noon and evening. Well, that's as it should be. And perhaps she's right. Maybe I should go there more often. But how to find the time? In our job one is always busy. And never more busy than that dreadful week!

'Madrid was on to me, Colonel Ramirez was on to me, the Legal Department was on to me – "Get those men processed!" they said. But there were hundreds of them! I didn't know which way to turn. I've only got a handful of men, and, between you and me, Señor, some of them are not great hands at paperwork. So it all fell on one or two. And me. And it wasn't until about the third day that I saw Señor Lockhart's name on the list.

25

'"Christ, what have you done?" I said. "There's a respectable man here!"

'"How were we to know he was respectable?" they protested. "We just took him in like everyone else!" And, you know, Señor, when I thought it over, I couldn't blame them. In the heat of the moment . . .

'"All right, all right!" I said. "But, boys," I said, "you've made a mistake. You've picked up someone who was nothing to do with it. Someone who'd popped out for a look –"
"But, boss," they said, "he *was* something to do with it. And he hadn't just popped out for a look. He'd been there all the time. We'd seen him."'

'Seen him doing what?' said Seymour.

'Talking. Talking to them. In a friendly way. Giving instructions, my men said. Telling them what to do.'

'How do they know that?' said Seymour.

'That's just what I asked them. They said they'd heard him. But, between you and me, Señor, I had my doubts. How anyone could hear anything in all that racket beats me. I said, "Look, lads, this is an important man and you've got to be sure. Sure enough to be able to stand up to a lawyer asking you twisty questions."

'Well, they weren't so sure then, and I wasn't so sure, either. All the same, I wasn't not sure, if you know what I mean. I mean, what the hell was he doing there? If he wasn't mixed up in it somehow?

'The fact was, we'd taken him in, and there he was in the prison, and that's no place for any respectable man to be. Particularly with all those hoodlums. So I sent a man down there post haste.

'But by the time he'd got there, Lockhart had already died. I was – well, I won't say I was distraught, I'm not that kind of man, you can't be in my job, but I was pretty cut up, I can tell you. "He's a decent man," I said to my wife, "and now – this!"

'Well, she thought a bit. "Yes, a decent man, yes," she said. "But he's also a big one. There will be questions asked about this. And you're going to have to find some answers." "I'll get down there right away," I said. "No," she said. "Don't you do that. All you did was pull him in. It's for others to answer questions about what happened afterwards."'

'But, just a moment,' said Seymour. 'Is it? He was in police custody when he died. Your custody.'

The Chief put his hand up. 'Ah, no, Señor. I must correct you on that. He wasn't in my custody.'

'Not in your custody?'

'No. You see, Señor, we had so many coming in that in no time at all our cells were full. So we had to send them straight down to the main jail. And that's where Señor Lockhart was taken. And where he died.'

'Ah, Señor Lockhart!' said the prison governor, shaking his head. 'A bad business, that! Tragic! One of the many tragic things that happened during Tragic Week. I couldn't believe it when I heard.'

'When you heard?' said Seymour. 'But surely you knew that he had been admitted?'

'No. Not straightaway. You have to understand, Señor, that hundreds were being admitted. We were swamped. It was days before we sorted ourselves out. And, besides, we weren't supposed to be doing the initial processing. That is normally the responsibility of the police. But everything was at sixes and sevens during that week. It took time to sort it out. And it was only when things were beginning to settle down that I heard that an Englishman had been admitted. And it was some time after that that I heard it was Señor Lockhart.

'"Señor Lockhart?" I said. "But that is ridiculous!" For Señor Lockhart is well known around here. Was well known, that is. I knew him myself. My wife knew him. Socially. I sent someone down immediately. But then they came back and told me he was dead. "Dead?" I said. "How can he be?" For all prisoners are looked at by a doctor when they are admitted. Now, as I said, we were all at sixes and sevens that week and there may have been a little delay. But he should have been seen by a doctor, and in fact he *was* seen by a doctor. Who should surely have spotted it if he had been wounded.

'I called him in at once. "What's this?" I said. "What sort of examination is this, when you can't even tell when a man's got a bullet in him?" "But, Governor," he said, "he *didn't* have a bullet in him!" "Oh, come," I said, "what did he die of, then?"

'"Shock," he said. "Heart failure. A stroke or something."

'"Or something." I said. "Look, you'll have to do better than that. This man was known to me personally. And to my wife. And to a lot of other people, too. Big people. People who'll put their boot up your backside. You'd better find out what he did die of. Pretty quickly, too."

'Well, he went off. And then next minute he was back. White as a sheet. "Boss," he said, "he was poisoned!"

'"Bollocks!" I said. "Now you go back and look again. And look a bit more carefully this time. Poisoned, my ass! Here? In my prison?"

'But, Christ, it was true. That was what the post-mortem showed. Poisoned! I couldn't believe it.'

'Was there an inquiry?' asked Seymour.

'Was there an inquiry?' the prison governor mimicked ironically. 'You bet there was! I told my deputy to get down there at once. And then I went over it myself. With a fine-tooth comb.'

'And did you find anything?'

'No,' the governor admitted.

'No?'

'No. Nothing hard, that is. Nothing that would stand up in court. The bastards were too clever. I had them in and grilled them. Personally. Myself. But there was no one we could actually tie it on to. They were too damned clever. Of course, we know who did it.'

'You know who did it?'

'The anarchists.'

'Anarchists?'

'The place was full of them. Especially after Tragic Week. It still is. That's the best place for them. Inside. Where they can't do any harm. At least, they shouldn't be able to do any harm. But –'

'You're saying you had some anarchist prisoners, and that they, or some of them, poisoned Señor Lockhart?'

'That's right.'

'But –'

'You wonder how this can be? I will tell you. Spain is a strange country just at the moment. It is full of anarchists. Yes! Anarchists. There is a strong popular movement. The Government is very worried. You can see how strong they are when you look at Tragic Week. A mass insurrection. Of anarchists. They came out on the streets. The Army had to be called out to put them down.'

'Anarchists?' said Seymour incredulously,

The governor was watching him.

'Yes, anarchists,' he said. 'I know you, coming from England, find this hard to believe. But it is true. The anarchist movement is very strong in Spain. And especially around Barcelona. They are all around us, Señor!'

'And in your prison, too, you say. But, surely, if Lockhart was in a cell with them, that narrows it down –'

The governor held up a hand. 'Ah, no. Let me correct you there, Señor Seymour. He had been in a cell with a lot of others, that is true. But then he was moved to a cell of his own.'

'He was in a cell of his own when he was poisoned?'

'That is correct, yes.'

'But –'

'Someone showed a flash of intelligence. They realized that he was an Englishman. "An Englishman?" they said. "What the hell is he doing here?" So they moved him.'

'Into a cell of his own?'

'Yes.'

'And that's where he died? Where he was poisoned?'

'Yes.'

'But – but how could that be? How could the poison have been got to him? The warders –'

Again the governor held up his hand.

'I know what you are thinking, Señor. And you are right, suspicion must fall on the warders. Or so you would think. But, Señor Seymour, here it is not like that. The prison was, as I say, full of anarchists. All in their cells. You would think it impossible for them. But, Señor, I'll tell you how it could happen.

'One day a warder is talking to a prisoner. That is allowed, yes? You cannot forbid people to talk. And the prisoner says, "Would you like a cigarette?" Well, yes. The warder would like a cigarette. What is wrong with that? Anyone may smoke. So he accepts a cigarette. And then another one the next day. And the next.

'And then one day the prisoner says to the warder, "It is unjust that I should smoke, and that you should smoke, but that poor man down the corridor, alone in that cell, should not." Well, maybe it is, thinks the warder. But rules are rules. It cannot be allowed, he says. "Not allowed?" says the prisoner. "Look, it's just a cigarette! That's not going to bring the Government down, is it? Let me just stick a hand in."

'"No, no, it cannot be done. It is forbidden." "To put a hand in? With a cigarette? For a poor man who is dying for a smoke? Have you no heart?" "Well, maybe just one," said the warder.

'But you see what has happened? The system has been subverted. A chink has been opened. Just a chink, but the chink becomes a crack, and through the crack anything can pass. Including poison.'

'All right,' said Seymour, 'I can see how it might have happened. But have you checked to see if it actually did happen?'

'Of course.'

'And?'

'And found nothing. Everyone on the corridor denies all knowledge.'

'And that is where it has been left?'

'Not left,' said the governor, hurt. 'An investigation was carried out. And is, in fact, still continuing.'

'Still continuing? But all this happened two years ago!'

'It takes time,' said the governor. 'There are many things to be considered.'

'But two years . . . When is the report expected?'

'Soon,' said the governor blandly. 'Soon.'

Oddly, Seymour knew about anarchists. The East End of London was full of them. You were always running into little anarchist groups, as you were into nutty groups of all kinds. The East End was an immigrant area. It was where you landed when you got off the boat. Where you landed and where, quite often, you stayed. Seymour's own family had done that. His grandfather had come first, from Poland, with his grandmother coming along a little later. Their son, Seymour's father, had grown up there and started a timber business. Later he had himself married another immigrant, this time from an obscure part of the Austro-Hungarian Empire. And that, in the East End, was where Seymour had been born, and where he had grown up, among the variety of immigrant families. This was how he had come to speak other languages. He had soon discovered that he had a flair for them. The police discovered that too and had put him to work mainly at first in the East End, among the people and languages that he knew.

Often the immigrants brought their enthusiasms and nuttinesses with them. Usually they were political nuttinesses, which was why they had had to emigrate in the first place. And, yes, there had been plenty of anarchists among them.

The newspapers, and, consequently, the politicians, often got excited about them. That in turn meant the police often got excited about them, too, and Seymour had frequently been put to work on the anarchist groups. He had soon found that they belied their reputation. Some were violent, certainly, but most of them weren't. Even with the violent ones, the violence was usually confined to their speaking. On the whole he had found them an unusually pacific lot.

So he knew about anarchists, yes. And he didn't believe a word of what the governor had been saying.

Before he left England Seymour had obtained Hattersley's Barcelona address and now he went to see him.

Hattersley jumped up from his desk.

'Seymour! You know, I had my doubts whether . . . When I was in London, I rather thought . . . That dreadful meeting! I wondered if I was wasting my time.'

'You certainly weren't.'

'I'm glad you think so. Now, what can I do for you? A drink?'

'Not just now, thank you. A few minutes of your time, that's all.'

'Glad to, glad to!'

And he seemed it. He was one of those men, Seymour thought, who were always taking up causes: enthusiastic, committed to whatever he had just taken up. A little diffident, too, lacking, ultimately, in confidence; although still determined.

'Can I just take you back to the starting-point of this whole business? That church. Where you saw the coffins.'

'A shock, I can tell you!' said Hattersley. 'When I saw them get out –'

'Yes, indeed. Now, I've been looking at that church. It still shows the signs, doesn't it? The soot on the doors – it must have been badly burnt during Tragic Week. Who by?'

'Who by?' Hattersley fingered his chin. 'Well, a lot of places were damaged at the time . . .' he said uncertainly.

'But why the church?'

'Does there have to be a why? Couldn't it have just been an accident?'

'It looks pretty deliberate to me. And if so, I wondered why. Were some of the insurrectionists particularly opposed to the Church?'

'Well, a lot of people in Spain are opposed to the Church. It's not like England, you know. The Church is more powerful, and because it's more powerful, more people are against it.'

'The anarchists?'

'Anarchists are certainly opposed to the Church.'

'Could it have been them, then? I gather there were a lot of anarchists on the streets.'

'Were there as many as all that? I think the newspapers sometimes exaggerate . . . But they could have done it, I suppose.'

'And that little ceremony you witnessed: who was responsible for that? Clearly not the anarchists, if they are so opposed to churches. And yet it seems quite an anarchist thing to do.'

'Local people, perhaps?'

'I'm sure there was an element of localness. Was it just that it was the local church?'

'Well, it *was* the local church. But it didn't seem very churchy to me. I mean, usually when there's a church service over here, there's a lot of business that goes with it – incense, bells, that sort of thing.' Hattersley thought for a moment. 'And I didn't see any clergymen. No,' he said definitely. 'I didn't see any priests at all.'

'So not particularly religious, then, even though it's a church. But possibly still chosen because it's local. And the local people here are Catalan, aren't they?'

'Yes.'

'A Catalan point, then, not an anarchist one? After all, a key factor in the uprising was the attempt to embark Catalan conscripts.'

'That's certainly true.'

'Would they have burnt the church? Probably not. But they might well have used it. Afterwards, for a kind of ceremony of remembrance. And the Church, which would, presumably, have had to have given permission, might well have been prepared to go along with it. Which they certainly wouldn't do if the organizers were anarchists.'

'So what is your point, old man?'

'Since I've been here I've heard a lot about anarchists. But not much about the Catalans.'

'They're all Catalan around here, old boy.'

'And yet,' said Seymour, 'if the authorities are to be believed, there's not a Catalonian Nationalist among them.'

Chapter Three

One of the things he had already noticed about Barcelona was the crocodiles.

Of children. They were everywhere. Little, disciplined processions, usually with a man in a long black cassock at the head of them, with, perhaps, another man in an ill-fitting dark suit walking behind.

Here was one now. A crocodile of boys had entered the square, big boys at the front, small ones at the rear, chivvied by two men in dark suits. They went straight across the square and turned up a side street.

A bell began to sound.

A moment later another crocodile appeared, exactly similar except that it consisted of girls, and with nuns in attendance. They marched swiftly along, hands neatly folded in front, eyes cast modestly down. It, too, disappeared up the side street and shortly afterwards the bell stopped ringing.

Since Nina was a woman he thought it likely that she taught at the school the girls came from, but he couldn't see any woman with them who was not a nun. Besides, the *cabezudo* had definitely said that she taught at a school that was in the square. But he couldn't see one.

Most schools he had seen in Barcelona were easily recognizable. They were like barracks. From the outside all you could see was a high – three storeys high – white, forbidding wall, with a shut door which a porter reluctantly opened. There was nothing like this in the square. All there was was the play area in the corner.

Later, he established that there were two rooms behind the play area but at the moment all he could see was the play space, which itself seemed a bit impromptu, consisting only of a few pieces of equipment and an area marked off by a foot-high fence of split logs roped together. But that, it turned out, was Nina's school. He had asked someone where the school was and they had pointed to it without hesitation.

The trouble was, he couldn't see a way in. There didn't seem to be a gate. Perhaps you just stepped over the fence? Seymour was reluctant to do that, however, because there were a lot of children milling around on the other side. He went up to the fence and looked around for someone to speak to. Finding no one, he eventually addressed one of the children.

'Nina? *Si!*' the child responded.

He pointed to the other side of the play area and then, seeing that Seymour was still standing there uncertainly, called out impatiently.

'Nina! Nina!'

A young woman emerged from the mass of children.

'*Si?*' And then, seeing Seymour and Chantale, came across to them.

'Señora, forgive me for interrupting you. I was wondering if it might be possible to have a word with you?'

'It is about a child joining the school?' she asked, her eye taking in Chantale beside him. 'You will have to talk to Esther about that.'

'No. It is not about that. It is about a friend of mine. An Englishman. His name is Lockhart.'

She seemed to go still. 'Lockhart?'

'You know him?'

'Of course I know him!' she said. She hesitated, and then made up her mind. 'Later,' she said. 'When the children have gone to their science lesson. About ten minutes.'

Then she turned sharply away and plunged into a pile of children.

Seymour and Chantale walked back across the plaza and found a bench in the shade of a palm tree. It didn't give much shade but they were glad of what there was. Already the heat in the square was building up.

They sat for a while watching the children. Although it seemed pretty hectic in the play area, it sorted itself out gradually into little areas of purposeful play, which they watched, amused.

Suddenly something was happening. The children had stopped playing and were going inside. There was another, older, woman with Nina, he saw now, and she went inside with them. Nina stayed behind and came across.

'Esther is taking them now,' she said. 'We have twenty minutes. You wished to talk to me about Lockhart.'

'My name is Seymour and I am a policeman from London. I have come to find out what happened to Lockhart.'

She nodded. Then she looked at Chantale.

'And this is Chantale. She is with me.'

She nodded again. 'You are from Algeria, Señora?'

'Morocco.'

'Lockhart knew many people from Algeria. That is why I thought . . . And from Morocco, too.'

'I am from Tangier.'

'Then you will understand why Lockhart went out into the streets that night.'

'That night in Tragic Week?' asked Seymour.

'Yes.'

'Señora, I do not know much about Lockhart yet but I get the impression from what you are saying that he felt concerned for the young men being sent out to fight in Africa?'

'That is so, yes. It was wrong; wrong that they were going at all, and wrong that they were being forced to go.'

'And Lockhart felt this strongly?'

37

She laughed, a little bitterly. 'Lockhart felt all things strongly.'

'Why did he go out into the streets?'

'To observe. And then bear witness. He thought that people would believe him afterwards, when they wouldn't believe us.'

'Because he was . . . outside it?'

'Because he was an Englishman. And therefore neutral.'

'Neutral between . . .?'

'The Government. The Army.'

'And . . .?'

'The people.'

'The Spanish people?'

'The Catalonian people. It was our men that they were sending out to fight. In their war.'

'And, if I have understood you correctly, Señora, there was another reason why Lockhart felt involved: he had strong sympathies, too, for those the soldiers were being sent against?'

'That is so, yes. He had lots of contacts with Algerians and Moroccans and looked upon them as his friends. "We get on well," he said. "Why do we need soldiers?" But he was thinking of the sort of relationships that go on without Government – private relationships, even business relationships. "Where there is Government, there is not relationship, but domination," he used to say. "The Spanish want to take over the country. Just as the French do, are doing, in both Algeria and Morocco."'

She gave a thin little smile. 'And as the British, everywhere. That was why he left Britain. He didn't like to think of himself as British. Except when it was useful.'

Something that the Admiral had said came into Seymour's mind and he was puzzled.

'You are suggesting that he turned his back on England, Señora?'

'Yes, of course.'

She looked at him almost triumphantly.

'But not on the Catalonians?'

'No.'

'Why was that?'

She looked surprised.

'Because we are an oppressed people,' she said seriously.

'Clearly he felt so,' Seymour said, 'if he was prepared to go out into the streets that night.'

'Yes.'

'And was that why the police picked him up? So that he wouldn't be able to bear witness?'

'I think they were as frightened as we were and didn't know what they were doing. They just picked everyone up, everyone who was there.'

'You say "we", Señora, does that mean that you yourself were there?'

'Yes.'

'But you weren't picked up?'

'Someone knocked me over, or I fell over. I lay there half stunned and then someone pulled me into a house.'

'But Lockhart was taken to prison. Where he died.'

'He was killed!' she said passionately. 'They killed him.'

'*After* he was taken into prison?'

'Yes.'

'Why?'

'They must have found out who he was.'

'He was known to them, then?'

'Lockhart was well known in Barcelona.'

'Forgive me, Señora, known for *what*?'

'Everyone knew him. He was always coming here on business.'

'For business, then; not for anything else?'

'What do you mean?'

'For, shall we say, his sympathies?'

She laughed, a short bark of a laugh. 'They knew his sympathies, too.'

'But that would not be enough, surely, for them to want to kill him?'

39

'It *ought* not to be enough. But, Señor,' she said bitterly, 'this is Spain.'

'Even so –'

'You have to understand, Señor, the kind of man that Lockhart was. It wasn't enough for him to believe something. If he believed something, he also had to *do* something.'

'He translated his beliefs into action?'

'Yes. Yes!'

'Catalonian beliefs? Catalonian action? But I thought you said, Señora, that he was neutral.'

'He was neutral about the fighting. Or not neutral. He felt it was wrong. But he also felt that it was wrong to force young men into the Army and then to send them to Africa.'

'Many would consider that stance laudable, Señora. I cannot believe that it would make a Government wish to kill him.'

'It wasn't just Catalonia.'

'What was it, then?'

She didn't reply for a moment but stood there thinking. Then she said: 'You have seen our school. What did you think of it?'

'Think of it?' said Seymour, surprised. 'Well . . .'

'Different,' said Chantale.

Nina seemed pleased.

'Yes,' she said, 'we are different. This is a Ferrer school. You know about Ferrer schools? No? I will tell you. There are a lot of them. Especially here, around Barcelona. They were founded by Francisco Ferrer. He called them Modern Schools. You know about this?'

'Well, I know what "modern" means . . .'

'No, no, that is not it. That is not it at all. He called them Modern to mark them off from other schools. In Spain, schools are under the Church, yes? His schools were not. They were . . . how shall I say? Rationalist, yes? *Not* religious. Not under the Church.' She paused for a moment, 'Free-thinking,' she said in English. 'Is that right?'

40

'Atheist?'

'*Si*. But that is not all. They were modern, too, in that the curriculum is modern. It includes, for example, science. In Church schools there is no science. It is frowned upon because it disturbs people. The Church does not like people to be disturbed. Nor does the Government, no?'

'Well, I suppose science helps you to see things in a different way –'

'Yes!' she said eagerly. 'That is it! And that is not allowed. Not in Spanish schools. It leads to children questioning. And if they question as children, they may continue to question as adults. That, say the authorities, we cannot have. In our schools. And so Ferrer started up his schools, different schools, which would offer an alternative. It is in the end a matter of freedom. Freedom from Church control. Freedom from control of all sorts! You have seen our school, yes? You have seen the children playing. It is free, yes? The children are happy, they are allowed to go their own way!'

'Yes, I do see that. At least, that is what I gather from a first impression. And you are rightly enthusiastic about your school. But – but – forgive me, Señora – what is all this to do with Lockhart?'

'The school was built with his money. He paid for the rooms, he bought the equipment. He helped to pay our wages. We need that because we are a private school and we have to charge. Oh, only a little, the families are poor, they can't afford much. But each one pays something. This is important because it says that they are not beggars. But we couldn't live on the money they give. So we wouldn't be here if it were not for Lockhart's money. *That* is why I say Lockhart was not content with just words. He always had to *do* something.'

'Well, that is very praiseworthy. As is his generosity. I always like people who are prepared to put their money where their mouth is. But, Señora, how does all this connect with his death? However strongly the Government might disapprove of his views on education, I cannot believe that –'

She cut him short impatiently. 'Still you have not understood! This is an *anarchist* school. Anarchist, yes? You understand *that*?'

'Of course I understand what anarchism is! But – look, I just can't believe that it would be enough for the Government to want to kill him!'

'Why wouldn't it be?' she demanded. 'It was enough to make the Government kill Ferrer. And that was in Tragic Week, too!'

Yes, Seymour knew about anarchists. And he thought he knew about Nina, too. He had met women like her in the political East End: serious, articulate and committed; and usually a great problem for the ordinary police constable to handle. He didn't know how to go about them. They didn't respond to the badinage which was part of the East End policeman's stock in trade, an essential tool in the soothing of relationships. They saw the badinage as sexual, which, admittedly, it often was, and took offence. In no time at all the policeman had bigger trouble on his hands, and he soon learned to give such women a wide berth.

Seymour didn't mind them. He quite liked talking to them. There was an element of seriousness in their conversation that he responded to. Partly it was his own family again. They were an argumentative lot and used to holding their own corners. Seymour's mother came from a revolutionary past in Herzegovina and his sister was a member of just about all the left-wing organizations that there were in the East End, and there were certainly plenty of those. She was a bit like Nina.

Sympathy, though, was one thing; credence quite another. He took what Nina said with a pinch of salt. He felt, though, that he had learned something about Lockhart. Several things, in fact. Perhaps there was more to the anarchist movement in Spain than he had supposed. And Lockhart seemed particularly prone to following his sympathies into all kinds of complicated political situations. The thought came to him that maybe the Deputy Commissioner had been right: this was not a thing for Scotland Yard. Or him personally. But, then, without that he wouldn't be here, would he? And if he weren't here, he wouldn't be with Chantale.

Hattersley had pressed him to return for a drink that evening. Seymour had hesitated, reluctant to abandon Chantale.

'I'm afraid I'm rather committed to a colleague,' he said apologetically.

'Bring him along! Yes, do!' said Hattersley enthusiastically.

'It's not a him, actually –'

'Bring her along! All the better!'

Colleague? How was he going to get out of this?

'Not – not a police colleague, actually.'

'No?'

Inspiration came. 'A colleague on the Intelligence side.'

'Really?' Hattersley was impressed. 'I suppose that will be on the Naval side,' he said. 'I must say, the Admiral has really got things moving!'

'Yes. Yes. Naval Intelligence. That's what she is.'

Foreboding struck him.

'But you'd better keep that quiet,' he said.

'Of course, old man! Of course. Hush hush. Absolutely! Not a word.'

Hattersley seemed slightly surprised, however, when he arrived with Chantale. He fussed around her and showed her out on to the balcony. But then he took Seymour aside and said: 'She's not quite what I expected, you know.'

'What did you expect?' said Seymour, with sinking heart.

'Well, not someone like this.' He caught himself up. 'Well, you wouldn't, would you? Not if they were in Naval Intelligence. I mean, if they were obviously Naval Intelligence, that wouldn't do at all. Give the game away, wouldn't it? Crafty old bugger, the Admiral! No one would think for a moment –'

'That's the idea, of course,' said Seymour.

'Of course! Of course!'

'You will keep quiet about it, won't you?'

'Oh, gosh, yes. I've always thought it was best to steer clear of these Intelligence things. Unlike Lockhart. He was pretty close to the Admiral at one time. Goodness knows what they got up to. But I think the Admiral found him pretty useful. Not for me, though. A bit too risky for me, that sort of thing.'

He took Chantale a gin-and-tonic and then came back to Seymour, still shaking his head.

'Well, she would certainly have fooled me! Pretty smart, is she?'

'Oh, gosh, yes,' said Seymour.

'One of their aces? Trust the Admiral to get one of the best!'

A little later, as they were sitting out on the balcony, Hattersley said, 'Excuse me, Miss de Lissac, do you mind my asking? Do you come from these parts?'

'Tangier,' said Chantale.

'Ah, Tangier? Well, you'll know your way around, then. I'm sure that's why they chose you. The Arab dimension! Well, I'm not going to say a word about that, of course. Not a word. It wouldn't have occurred to me, but I daresay the Admiral knows what he's doing.'

Then he slapped his hand on his knee.

'Of course!' he said. 'Stupid of me not to spot it! The Arab dimension! Important with Lockhart. Always was.'

'Why should that be?'

Hattersley smiled. 'Well, he married one, for a start.'

'His wife was an Arab?'

'Yes. Leila,' said Hattersley. He chuckled. 'Leila Lockhart. Double L. That made her Welsh, Evans said. You don't know Evans, do you? A bit of a wag. You don't see him much over here but you'd see him every day in the Club over in Gibraltar. Great joker! "Ll" as in Llangollen. Very good, don't you think?'

'Ye-e-es . . .'

'Well, I thought so. And so did Leila. She laughed no end.'

'Yes. Yes, I'm sure. And – and she's running the business now, I gather?'

'Yes. Took over when Sam died. Of course, she knew all about it. Knew more than he did, Sam used to say. A tough old bird, Leila. Wily, too. She'll be a match for them.'

'Match for . . .?'

'The Spaniards. They always give you trouble if you're trading out of Gibraltar. Between you and me, that's why I've got a sub-office here. Why Sam had one, too.'

'Difficult, were they? The Spaniards?'

'Oh, yes. Mind you, it didn't bother Sam too much. It was part of the game, he said. He quite liked them, actually. More than they liked him, the bastards. He used to say they were a proud people and that was why they were so difficult. Like the Arabs, he said. Proud. That's what people didn't recognize. But he could understand them, he said, because the Scots were like that. But not the English.

'Well, of course,' said Hattersley, 'I took him up on that. "What about our Navy?" I said. "We're proud of that. And our cricket. Sometimes." "No, no," he said, "it's not the same thing. You've got to be touchy with it. The English aren't touchy because they take their superiority for granted. The Spaniards can't, because they lost their superiority long ago. The Arabs even longer. So they're touchy, and that makes them difficult." Sam said he didn't mind that because he could understand it.'

45

'Yes. Yes, I see. Interesting theory. Possibly. And – and he was married to an Arab, you say?'

'Yes. He met her when he was over there once. Married her and brought her back to Gibraltar, and they've stayed together ever since. Just!'

Hattersley laughed. 'There were some rocky moments, especially early on. Sam's always had a roving eye and it roved a bit too frequently for Leila. There was even talk of a child he'd had by some other woman, which made things harder. They couldn't seem to manage any children of their own, you see. And I think she found it very difficult at first in Gibraltar. It was a bit too British and stiff-upper-lip for her. But, then, there are always stresses and strains in a mixed marriage, aren't there?'

'Yes,' said Chantale.

'You spoke of an Arab dimension to Lockhart,' Seymour said. 'Did it go further than just the fact that he was married to one?'

'Oh, yes,' said Hattersley. 'A lot of his business was over there. That's how he first made his name. Started there. In Algeria, I think. And then spread along the coast. And then came back to Gibraltar. But he always kept up that side. It had grown quite big by the time he left. That's where he made the bulk of his money, in fact. Of course, Leila's family are there. That's why he married her, some say. But I don't believe that. Leila was always first with him. No matter what happened, he always went back to her.

'I asked him once why he didn't stay out there. "Gibraltar's become too important to me now," he said. It was the Navy, you see. Especially when the Admiral took over. He needed help, you see. Especially over the oil business – when the ships converted to oil. He had to scratch around a bit for supplies, and that's where Lockhart, with his contacts, came in. It's not so important now, of course, but it gave Lockhart a leg up, and that's all he needed. The firm still does a lot of work for the Navy. That's why the

Admiral got so fired up when Lockhart was killed. He wouldn't have got Whitehall interested without him.'

Hattersley looked at Chantale.'I don't expect I'm telling you much you don't know, Miss de Lissac. I'm pretty sure that the Arab dimension was at the back of his mind when he asked for an Arabic speaker. And why Naval Intelligence is interested. But I won't say another word about that. I promise!'

'You see,' said Chantale, as they walked away. 'I'm pretty important.'

'I always thought you were,' said Seymour.

'To *work*,' said Chantale, with emphasis. 'To your work. Remember it? It's why you came.'

'It's not why I came,' said Seymour.

Before they settled on a restaurant for the evening, Chantale and Seymour joined the rest of Barcelona in the regular evening promenade along Las Ramblas. The lights had come on in the trees and with them Barcelona had suddenly come to life.

The *cabezudos* were out again, gambolling like, and often with, children. They gave them rides on their backs, capering with their heels and throwing up their rear ends like bucking broncos. The children squealed and clung tight to the giraffe-like necks. However, they were seldom in real danger of falling. These were friendly *cabezudos*.

Seymour tried to work out which one had spoken to him. He would like to talk more. But no *cabezudo* approached him. If anything, the *cabezudos* seemed more interested in Chantale. 'Scratch my back, Señora!' pleaded one of them, rubbing itself against a palm tree.

Laughing, Chantale declined the invitation.

'Go on, Señora!' said someone in the crowd. 'It will bring you luck.'

The *cabezudo* skipped up to her and presented its back. Chantale put her hand out.

'That's it, Señora! Oh, lovely lady, do it again!'

'You want to watch out, Señora,' said a woman laughing. 'Or else it will run away with you.'

'My mother ran away with a *cabezudo*,' declared a *cabezudo* capering nearby. 'And look what happened!'

'Oh, that's nice!' said Chantale's *cabezudo*. 'Now behind the ears, lovely lady!'

'Next thing, it will be between its legs,' said a woman in the crowd.

Chantale stepped back hurriedly.

'Mother of God!' cried the *cabezudo* indignantly. 'The minds these women have!'

'Take no notice of him,' advised another *cabezudo*, sidling up to Chantale. 'Scratch my back instead!'

'No, no! Scratch mine! I've got a much better back,' cried another *cabezudo*, rushing up.

'Back, did he say?' said the women in the crowd, which was now enjoying the occasion hugely.

In a moment, all the *cabezudos* came round them.

'Did you talk to Nina?' came a hiss from behind Seymour's back.

'Yes. Thank you. Can we talk somewhere?'

The *cabezudos* began to dance round him in a circle. He tried to make out which one had spoken.

One of the *cabezudos* was carrying a fish. He dangled it before Seymour's eyes.

'Do you like fish, Señor?'

'Lockhart did,' breathed the familiar voice behind him.

'Would I be wise to?'

'Oh, yes.'

'Then yes.'

'Try this, then,' said the *cabezudo* with the fish, now behind him, catching him a buffet with it across the ear.

Seymour spun round but the *cabezudos* spun with him.

'Lockhart would get them fresh,' whispered the familiar voice.

'Fresh?'

'From the sea.'

The *cabezudos* danced away and formed a ring round Chantale. They presented their backs and began rubbing themselves up against her.

'You had better look to your lady, Señor,' said someone warningly.

Seymour grabbed Chantale and pulled her way.

'These *cabezudos* need a cold bath!' he said to the crowd.

'Or a bucket of water thrown over them,' said the jolly woman who had joined in the back chat before.

She was a stout, matronly woman with a large coloured shawl thrown over her head. Chantale took refuge between her and Seymour and the *cabezudos* danced off to find another victim.

'Those *cabezudos*!' said the woman. 'They're becoming impossible!'

'They've always been like that,' said someone else.

'But now they're worse!' insisted the stout lady.

'It's the times,' the other person said. 'When the times are bad, they become unruly.'

'They say things that should not be said,' said the stout lady.

'But maybe they need saying,' said someone in the crowd.

'Maybe they do,' conceded the stout lady, 'but sometimes they go too far.'

'Sometimes they say things, though, that are helpful,' said Seymour.

The stout lady gave him a quick look.

'Be warned, Señor; they are not always to be trusted. What seems helpful may not be so.'

Chapter Four

It was early in the morning and although there were one or two people sitting in the café the chairs were still tipped against the tables outside. Dolores was going round tipping them back and wiping the tops of the tables. She recognized Seymour and greeted him politely but warily.

He sat down at one of the tables outside, where no one would hear them, and asked for a coffee. When she brought it, he said:

'Dolores, I would like some advice.'

'From me?' she said, surprised. She thought for a moment and then said, 'Well, my advice would be for you to go back home.'

'Would you like that?'

She considered. 'No. But it's good advice.'

'I've been to the prison,' Seymour said, 'and I've got nowhere.'

'Well, that's a surprise.'

'I talked to the governor. I want to talk to people lower down. Other prisoners. People who were there when Lockhart died and who might know something about it.'

'I can't help you,' said Dolores, dabbing at the table.

'Can't?' said Seymour. 'Or won't?'

'Look,' said Dolores. 'I've got a life to live and I want to live it. Lockhart told me to stay out of it and I reckon he knew what he was doing. Because he didn't and now he is dead. I don't want to be like that. Manuel said the same.'

'It's about Manuel that I want to talk.'

'About *Manuel*?' she said, surprised.

'Yes. You said that when you couldn't get into the prison to see Lockhart, Manuel said he would fix it. And later he did. Could he do that for me, do you think?'

'No. He did it for me because I was one of his girls. He looks after us waitresses, you know, and he knew how things were between me and Lockhart. He wouldn't do it for just anybody.'

'This is still Lockhart.'

'It's not the same.'

'If you asked him.'

'He knows that Lockhart is dead. And he's said, "Now that he's dead, forget him."'

'You can't forget him, though, can you?'

She moved away and began polishing a little vigorously.

'No,' she whispered. 'No, I can't.'

'You told me to see the people in England did not forget him, either. I'm doing that. But I need help. Will you help me?'

She moved away to another table.

He waited but she did not come back.

He finished his coffee and got up to go, putting some coins on the table. At the last moment she came back.

'Why don't *you* ask him?' she said. 'He knows you've come from England and that you want to know about Lockhart. You could say you were asking on behalf of Lockhart's father. Manuel is very keen on fathers. He never had one himself and he has this idealistic picture. I'll take you in to him and say that you've come to me and I don't know what to do.'

'Ah, Señor,' said Manuel, 'it is too late now. No one can do anything.'

His large brown eyes looked at Seymour sadly. He had a big droopy face and, with the eyes, the effect was of a large, doleful spaniel.

'I know,' said Seymour. 'Nevertheless, the father –'

'Ah, the father,' sighed Manuel.

Seymour took him confidentially by the arm. 'All I can hope to do is set his mind at peace.'

'Of course. Of course!'

'It is the uncertainty that is tearing him apart. All he knows is that his son has disappeared in a foreign country. He cannot believe that he is dead. How could he be? How could such a thing happen? In a country like Spain? It must be a mistake.

'Someone has spoken of prison. But how can that be? His son, he knows, is no criminal. It is, surely, a mistake. A clerical error. You know these clerks, you know these bureaucrats. Well, it will be the same in Spain as it is in England. Some fool of a clerk has got it wrong. It *must* be so! And so he goes on tearing himself apart.

'If I could find out something for sure, then perhaps that would help him. If it was only to confirm that he was dead. At the moment, you see, he cannot believe that he *is* dead. He goes on hoping that he is still alive. And he will until he knows for sure.'

'Alas,' said Manuel sympathetically, 'there can be no doubt.'

'But told in a notification from a prison! Cold, bald, remote. Can it be relied on? An institution – big, heartless, and, perhaps, like so many institutions, wrong. A mistake – that's what it could be! And while there's a chance of that he will go on hoping. Until – you will understand this, I am sure, Señor – some personal witness . . . a human being, someone of flesh and blood, not an anonymous cipher in an anonymous institution . . . says it definitely.

'Well, that is all I am hoping for, Señor, all I can expect to achieve. Will you help me, Señor, in this task I am undertaking for a bereft, deeply loving father?'

'Señor, I will! For the sake of the holy bond that exists between father and son, I will!'

* * *

Lockhart's Barcelona office was just round the corner from the church with soot-blackened doors through which the coffins had emerged. It was up a side street at the entrance to which several Arabs were lounging. They looked curiously at Chantale and for a moment she wondered if she should put her scarf back over her face; but then she decided she would not, and looked back at them hard, and after a moment they looked away.

Seymour registered that but registered also, with his policing experience, that they posed no threat. This was Spain and without the reinforcement they would have received from the general culture in Morocco or Algeria their power dwindled and they seemed slightly helpless.

The office consisted of two rooms and a man at a desk. The man was Arab, too.

'I am looking for Señor Lockhart's office,' said Seymour.

'This is it. But Señor –'

'I know,' said Seymour. 'But the business goes on? Who runs it now?'

'His wife. From Gibraltar. That's where the main office is. This is just a branch office.'

'So you're on your own here?'

'I always was on my own. Mr Lockhart used to come over from time to time but mostly he left me to get on with it.'

'And, of course, he was over here when – well, during Tragic Week.'

'Yes.'

'And you were, too, presumably?'

'Yes.'

'What was it like?'

'Terrible, terrible. After the first day we all kept inside. I kept inside here. For five nights I did not go home. "You stay right here, Hussein," he told me. "I'll see food comes in. Don't even put your head out."'

'But he did. He went out, didn't he? Into the streets.'

'Yes.'

'Why was that?'

'To look after his friends.'

'Friends?'

'Arab friends. We thought at first, when it began, that it was directed against us. It usually is.'

'But it wasn't this time, was it? It was the conscripts.'

'Yes, but we didn't know that. Not at first. And when we did, people began to come out on their side. So in the end it didn't make any difference. I don't suppose it would have anyway. Once the Army had been called in, they would have gone for us anyway.'

'And Lockhart was trying to see they didn't?'

'Yes.'

'Wasn't that foolhardy? I mean, one man –'

'He was well known. He thought he had influence. He thought he might be able to stop them. Just being there, he thought, an independent witness, it might restrain them.'

'But it didn't?'

'No. And it was foolish to even think that he could. But Señor Lockhart was like that. Foolhardy, yes. But generous, too. And he thought that nothing could happen to him. That he was, somehow, inviolable. That the bullets wouldn't touch him. But they always do, don't they?'

'Except that, apparently, this time they did not. He was just taken into prison.'

'The bullet got him in the end, though, didn't it?'

'Was it a bullet?'

The Arab shrugged.

'The garrotte, perhaps?' he offered.

There were flies buzzing in the window and through an open door Seymour could see Arabs sitting in an upper room. They were sitting on the ground, squatting on their haunches, content to sit in the darkness, since that was cooler. It could have been Tangier, he thought.

'Why would they do that?' he said.

The Arab shrugged again. 'To warn, perhaps? To warn others not to be too friendly?'

54

He suddenly seemed to become nervous at his own frankness.

'Who are you?' he said.

'I'm British,' said Seymour. 'Like Lockhart. A British policeman. Lockhart had British friends. Who are wondering what happened to him.'

'A policeman?' said the Arab doubtfully.

'A British one,' said Seymour.

'Not Spanish?'

'No.'

The Arab seemed relieved.

'The Spanish police came here,' he said. 'They wanted to know things about him. But we wouldn't say anything.'

'What might you have said?'

But the Arab did not reply.

Or perhaps he did.

'Lockhart had many friends,' he said.

'Arab friends?'

'*Si*.'

'I would like to meet some of those friends.'

The Arab thought.

'You *are* British?' he said, as it seeking reassurance.

'Yes. Cannot you hear it?'

The Arab smiled.

'Just,' he said.

Afterwards, Seymour thought that there was something strange about it: an Arab testing an Englishman's facility in Spanish. But the Arab seemed to see nothing strange in it. Perhaps he thought of himself as Spanish? He certainly spoke Spanish like a native and seemed confident of his ability to judge Seymour's Spanish.

'Whenever Señor Lockhart came down here,' he said, 'he always used to go to a particular café to play dominoes.'

'Where would I find it?'

'It's further on along the Calle. On the left.'

'A name, perhaps?'

The Arab hesitated.

'Mine is Seymour.'

'You could try asking for Ibrahim.'

As they were going out, the Arab looked at Chantale as if seeing her for the first time. Perhaps he *was* seeing her for the first time. When in the presence of women, Arabs often didn't seem to notice them. This was not necessarily rudeness; indeed, to them it was politeness. It was felt offensive to address a woman directly, almost shockingly so, if she was with her husband – as, Seymour suspected, Chantale might well be supposed to be.

'The Señora, perhaps, knew Lockhart?'

'Not directly,' said Chantale.

'The Señora –' there it was again, the obliqueness – 'is perhaps from Algeria?'

'Tangier.'

'Ah, yes. Señor Lockhart knew many people in Tangier.'

Seymour wondered if he could make use of Chantale's Arabness when he went to the café. Perhaps her being an Arab would in a way vouch for him. He suggested she go with him.

Chantale said it wouldn't do at all. Arab women never entered cafés, even with their menfolk. It was a very bad idea.

Seymour had to accept this but he was reluctant to abandon the idea altogether. As a foreigner, he felt he needed some kind of entrée into the Arab world, some kind of guarantee that he was a friend. He knew from experience that with immigrants this would be especially important.

In the end they decided that she would not go into the café with him but they would establish the link outside. They would go into the quarter together and then part. Chantale would go to the little market and make some purchases, as if shopping for a family. Seymour meanwhile would go into the café alone. When she had finished making her purchases she would stand outside the café patiently waiting for him. That, she said, ought to clinch it!

The café was set slightly below ground, as was usually the case with Arab coffee houses, and to enter it you had to go down some steps. Inside, it was dark. It was the Arab way to retreat from the sun and heat. There were stone benches around the wall and men were sitting on them either drinking coffee from small enamel cups or puffing away at bubble pipes on the ground beside them.

The men were all Arabs and Seymour at once felt himself to be, or was made to feel, an intruder. He sat down, however, in a corner with a low table in front of him. It was some time before he was served, one of those ways in which a café can make a customer feel he is not wanted. But then a waiter came up and put a cup before him and poured coffee from a coffee pot with a long spout.

As he bent over the table, Seymour said, 'Is Ibrahim here?'

The waiter inclined his head towards a man with a square-cut beard sitting with two men playing dominoes.

'Would you whisper a name in his ear? The name is Lockhart.'

The waiter showed no sign of having heard and continued on his round with the pot. Shortly afterwards, however, Seymour saw him bending over the man with the beard. The man sat up with a start. A little later Seymour saw him studying him carefully. Eventually he came across.

'You wish to speak with me?'

'About Lockhart.'

'Lockhart is dead.'

'I know. That is what I want to talk to you about.'

The Arab hesitated but then slid on to the bench beside Seymour.

'Who gave you my name?' he said.

'Hussein. The man in Lockhart's office.'

'Who are you?'

'My name is Seymour and I come from England.'

'From England?' said the man, astonished. 'Why?'

'Lockhart had friends there.'

'He had friends here. But —'

'They are interested in how he came to die.'

'We, too, are interested in how he came to die. But what business is it of theirs?'

'Naturally, as friends —'

The Arab shook his head firmly. 'It is no business of people in England.'

'Well, it *is*,' Seymour insisted. 'When an Englishman dies in a Spanish prison, the English Government is always interested.'

'This is nothing to do with Governments.'

'Did he not die in prison?'

'Well, yes, but —'

'And how did he come to be there? Was not *that* something to do with Government?'

'I do not think —' began the Arab, but stopped.

'And was he not taken in in Tragic Week when so many others were taken in? Including Arabs? And isn't *that* something to do with Government?'

'Yes. But it had nothing to do with Lockhart.'

'Nothing to do with Lockhart?' said Seymour, astonished.

'No. It was a terrible thing. But it was quite separate.'

'But did not Lockhart go out on to the streets so that he could bear witness?'

'Well, yes, and that was the act of a good man. But that was not why he died.'

'Why *did* he die, then?'

The Arab was silent for a while. Then he said, 'Señor, this is really no concern of yours. Nor of people in England. It is a private matter.'

'Private!'

'Yes. To him, to us.'

'As friends you may think that. But if the Government –'

The Arab shook his head. 'This was nothing to do with the Government, either Spanish or British. It was, as I have told you, a private matter. That it happened during Tragic Week was, well, incidental. The confusion of Tragic Week provided them with an opportunity. But even then they couldn't take it. They had to wait until he was in prison. Then it became easier.'

'Easier?' said Seymour incredulously. 'To kill a man when he is in prison?'

'Yes. Because then he didn't have his bodyguard with him.'

'What is this about a bodyguard?'

'You don't know about his bodyguard? No? Well, he had one. And they were very good, too. My people. People from the Rif. Good fighters, no nonsense. They would have protected him. But, of course, when he was in prison –'

'Why did he need a bodyguard? Who was it against?'

'Señor, you ask too many questions, when, really, this is no concern of yours. Go home to England. Leave it to us. We shall see that justice is done.'

He rose to his feet, took Seymour by the arm, and then escorted him firmly to the door. As they stepped up on to the street he caught sight of Chantale, waiting patiently outside, and stopped suddenly.

'Is she with you?' he said, surprised.

'Yes.'

The Arab looked uneasy.

'Are you from Leila?' he asked her.

'Leila? Lockhart's wife? No.'

The Arab looked again at Chantale, as if he did not believe her.

'I was thinking of going to see her, though,' said Seymour.

The Arab shook his head.

'I do not think that would be wise,' he said.

'Why not?'

The Arab disregarded his question. He kept studying Chantale, as if fascinated. 'Why have you come here, Señora?' he said abruptly.

Chantale, not unnaturally, was caught for a reply.

'Because she must,' said Seymour.

'I have come to find out,' said Chantale, cleverly.

'Leave it to us, Señora. This is not for women. Go back to your own people.'

'Who are her people?' said Seymour.

The Arab looked at him.

'Yes,' he said. 'That is the question, isn't it? For all of us.'

Seymour and Chantale went for a walk along Las Ramblas. There was a slight breeze, which was very welcome because it was getting towards noon and the heat was already becoming overwhelming. The sunlight seemed to bounce back off the white boulevard. The flowers around the foot of the trees wilted. The onions on their strings seemed to hang more heavily. The piles of melons which had earlier shone green and gold seemed to whiten and lose their glow. The boulevard began to empty.

They found a little restaurant in a back street just off Las Ramblas. It was a humble place, consisting just of bare tables crammed together cheek by jowl, with the legs of the chairs often so interlocking that you could not get up or sit down without disturbing everyone else. But that did not seem to matter. It soon became apparent that most of the people there knew each other. Often they had children with them, who would crawl under the tables to escape or return. No one seemed to mind. In fact, the children appeared to be generally owned. Sometimes when they were very small and creating a hullabaloo an apparent stranger would reach over from one of the adjacent tables with a piece of bread dipped in sauce and give it to the child. Usually it worked and the child would calm down.

Once they had got used to the hubbub, Seymour and Chantale rather enjoyed it. There was so much of human interest going on. And somehow the family atmosphere was just what they needed at the moment.

A man in yellow oilskins came up carrying a bucket of freshly caught fish and the proprietor came out to study them.

'That's fine,' he said, 'that's fine. But, look, people are asking for sea bass tonight. We've got some coming up from the market but we'll need more. Can you get us some?'

'I'll ask Juan, and Silvia will bring them up if he's got any. I want to go out.'

'The fishing will be good tonight, will it?'

'Yes, God willing.'

'Or maybe you've got something else in mind,' said the proprietor, laughing.

'There is that,' said the oilskinned man.

'Well, just be careful, that's all.'

The proprietor took the bucket inside and the man in oil-skins waited for his return.

'Got time for a quick one?' asked someone at one of the tables, holding up a glass.

'Not just now, Vincente,' said the man in oilskins respectfully.

'Oh, it's like that, is it? Well, good luck!'

The proprietor came out again with the empty bucket and the man in oilskins took it and went off.

There was a noisy group just beside them and Seymour and Chantale couldn't quite make out what it was. In the end they decided that there had been a family christening and these were the family elders gathered to wet the baby's head. Someone had produced a huge camera and set it up nearby and began to take a photograph of the group. It was taking some time. The photographer's head disappeared under the cloth and he held up a hand. At the last moment a woman gave a cry, and the proceedings stopped while she took the bottles of olive oil and whatever off the table. She put them under the table so they would be out of the line of vision. Then the group recomposed itself. The photograph was taken and normal business resumed.

Then, suddenly, there was a dismayed cry. The woman, forgetting about the condiments, had kicked them over with her foot and now there was a great pool under the table and everyone was lifting their feet and inspecting their trousers and dresses.

The woman squeezed herself out and ran to one of the waiters to get a cloth. The waiter stood with arms akimbo and said with mock severity, 'Don't worry, I'll just stay on for a few hours and clean it up!'

The offender began apologizing profusely. Suddenly the waiter collapsed into laughter and put his arms around her. Everyone in the restaurant roared. A couple of waiters darted over with cloths and a bucket and began wiping the people down. The owner of the café appeared, chuckling, and suggested that the women go out into the kitchen and take their dresses off. 'What, again?' said someone, and everyone burst into laughter. 'She can save that till later,' someone said, and again the place erupted.

It seemed a very jolly place, not at all like the café Seymour had previously been to. But this was Spanish, he could tell by the voices. That had been Catalan. The only Catalan voice that he had heard here had been that of the fisherman.

At the back of the restaurant was a large metal fish tank. He got up and went over to it. At this time of the day there were only a few fish in it, but a huge pair of lobsters, armour-plated dinosaurs with whiskers like aerials, probing out in front of them.

'There'll be more this evening,' said a passing waiter. 'Last night's catch hasn't come in from the fish market yet. They'll be bringing it up right now.'

'Fresh from the sea, is it?'

'Straight from the boats. You can go down and see them if you want.'

'Boats?'

'Just through there. You wouldn't think it, with the docks so close, but there's a little harbour there for the fishing boats. It's a nice little place. You want to take a look.'

'Perhaps we will.'

'Down that street and keep going. Eventually you'll get there.'

Eventually they did, having almost lost their way in what became a maze of tiny side streets, where all the businesses were to do with the docks and the sea. In the doorways thigh-length rubber boots were hanging, with coils of rope and great drifts of netting. There was a carpenter's, where they were working on a boat, and a place where they were mending netting. And everywhere there was the smell of fish and tar and the sea.

The harbour was very small, just round a headland from the main docks for the cargo vessels, not an adjunct but a kind of afterthought, although it had probably been there longer than the docks. It was full of little fishing boats. They would be ones which fished locally and would be out at night. Just now it was deserted, apart from a solitary man pulling a long net up from a boat and running it through his fingers before folding it neatly on the quay. When they got closer they saw it was the man in yellow oilskins they had seen earlier.

They stopped for a moment and watched him.

The net must have been about fifty yards long and it was about a yard wide. As the man ran it through his fingers he pulled out seaweed and tar and little dead fishes and squid.

'Getting it ready for this evening?' said Seymour.

The man grunted.

'You've got to have it just right,' said Seymour.

'Sometimes it gets torn,' said the man. 'It fouls on

63

something. And then in no time you've got a hole as long as my arm and anything can get through.'

'What do you do? Tie it between buoys?'

'Sink it. I use buoys but this net needs to go deeper. I leave it for a couple of hours and then pull it in.'

'How far out do you go?'

'About two miles.'

'Don't you have to look out for the big boats coming in?'

The fisherman laughed.

'They don't come in until the morning,' he said. 'And do you know why?'

'Safety?'

The man laughed again. 'It's the Customs people. They don't like it. They like to have a good sleep during the night and save their work for the morning. So everyone has to wait.'

He spat contemptuously into the sea. 'The big boats lie offshore. So when I'm out there I just keep a bit further in. But sometimes they're so close I can hear them talking.'

'Or talk to them?'

The man gave him a long look.

'Or talk to them,' he agreed.

He bundled the net, neatly coiled now, up in his arms, took it across the quay, and dropped it into a boat. Then he walked off up the hill into the houses.

Seymour watched him go.

'Lockhart liked fish,' he said.

Chapter Five

'Inspector –?'

From inside the guardroom at the entrance to the Navy docks came a stifled gasp.

'Seymour from Scotland Yard.'

'Jesus!' Again from inside.

The seaman checking Seymour's papers suddenly looked rattled.

'Excuse me, sir.'

He dashed into the guardroom.

Through the open window Seymour could hear concerned discussion. Then:

'Well, you go out, sonny, and ask him who he wants to see.'

The seaman reappeared. 'Sorry, sir, just a minor point. I have to check. Who was it you wanted to see?'

'Admiral Comber.'

An unmistakable 'Christ!' came through the open window.

'Yes, sir. I'll get someone to take you over.'

He disappeared back into the guardroom. Seymour, left standing there alone, moved over to be nearer the window.

'You're for it, now, Ferry!' said a jaunty young voice.

'Christ, they've brought the narks in!' said another, older, coarser voice.

'I wonder why that could be?' said the young voice innocently. 'Something to do with the stores, do you think? You're looking a bit green, Ferry. Are you feeling all right?'

'Yes, sir. Thank you. Sir.'

'Ground moving in the stores, is it? Rough swell? Don't worry, Ferry, he'll just want to look at your records. And see how they match up to the stores on the shelves. That should be no problem, should it? Ferry, you really *are* looking rather green. Were you thinking of reporting sick, by any chance?'

'As a matter of fact, sir –'

'I'd hang on a bit if I were you,' continued the voice mercilessly. 'You don't want to draw attention to yourself, do you?'

'No, sir.'

'He won't be bothered by a few discrepancies, anyway.'

'That's right, mate,' the coarser voice chipped in encouragingly. 'Small things are not going to bother him.'

'It's the big things he'd be looking for,' said the jaunty one. 'Just big things. Ferry, you *are* looking a bit off-colour. I'll see if I can get something done about the heat in the stores. That *is* the problem, isn't it?'

'A bit hot, sir, yes. Just at the moment.'

'Don't worry, mate. He won't know if things are ship-shape or if they're not!'

'And they will be shipshape, won't they?' continued the merciless one, who seemed to be some sort of superior. 'By the time he gets there? I think if I were you, Ferry, I'd get along to the stores pretty smartish.'

'Yes, sir, I will, sir. If you don't mind –'

'Sir, he's still waiting outside,' said the seaman who had been checking Seymour's papers.

'Thank you, Parsons. We'd better get someone to take him over. In fact, I'll take him over myself.'

The seaman came out, accompanied by a midshipman who looked about fifteen years old. He put out a hand.

'Hello, Mr Seymour. I'm McPhail. The Duty Officer just at the moment. I'll take you over to see the comber eel right away.'

'Comber eel?'

'That's what we call him. The Admiral. But that's un-officially. Nice to meet you, Inspector. Are you going to help us solve our problems?'

'I doubt it,' said Seymour.

The midshipman laughed. 'Well, we start level, then. Because I don't think we're going to solve them, either.'

The seaman raised the bar which had been across the entrance.

'Sorry about all this,' said McPhail. 'It's not as if some-one's going to come in and pinch a ship.'

'Where are the ships?'

'Mostly out at sea. Wish I was, too. But there's a corvette in over there, and, just around the corner, a Navy tanker. Nothing much just now. Are you familiar with ships, Mr Seymour?'

'Not really. I occasionally have jobs in the docks, though.'

'Ah, do you? You'll know your way around this sort of place, then?'

'I wouldn't say that.'

But then, deciding to add to the stir:

'A bit about Purchasing, perhaps.'

'Ah, Purchasing?' He raised his voice: so that it would carry to the guardroom. 'You know about Purchasing, do you?'

Seymour thought he heard a faint groan.

'And stores,' he said.

'Stores, too? Oh, that will be very helpful!'

Seymour laughed. 'I'm not sure everyone will think so.'

McPhail laughed, too.

'You won't find anything too awful,' he said. 'But it won't half do them good if they think that you might.'

He pointed to a large building with long windows look-ing out to sea.

'That's the mess. The officers' mess. The wardroom, we call it. I expect the Admiral will take you over for a drink. Are you putting up there, while you're here?'

67

'No, I've booked in at a *pension*. The Pension Francia.'

McPhail looked doubtful. 'The Francia? Well, a lot of our people do stay there. When they're with a lady friend. Or wife, of course. Ladies can't stay in the mess. But the Francia is very handy.'

'It's that sort of place, is it?' said Seymour.

'I'm afraid so.'

'So you've come over to Gibraltar, then?' said the Admiral.

'Yes. There are several things I want to do. But it might be helpful if I could pretend to be investigating something else. You remember we spoke of the stores.'

'Fine. I'll set it up.'

'I've already dropped a few hints.'

'That probably accounts for the worried look on one or two faces.'

'If you can arrange things, I'll make a start. But that, of course, is not the real reason why I am here. Nor, I imagine, for your interest in Lockhart.'

'No.'

'What *is* the real reason for your interest in Lockhart?'

'I don't know how far I can go . . .'

'I've done a lot of Diplomatic work.'

'The man from the FO said you had, and that's good. But this isn't quite Diplomatic work.'

'I didn't think for a moment that it was.'

'No.'

The Admiral rubbed his chin. The bristles made a slight scrapy noise. Probably been up for hours, thought Seymour. Shaved in the middle of the night.

'No,' the Admiral said again. 'Defence is not the same as Diplomatic. Especially at the moment, when we might be in the run-up to another war.'

'You think so?'

'You always have to think so if you're in the Services. Especially if you're in the Navy. You've got to think that

68

far ahead. Do you know how long it takes to get one of our capital ships on a new course? One of the big ones? Well, you won't do it in much less than three-quarters of a mile. So it's no good coming up at the last moment and saying, "Mind that boat!" Or rock, or whatever. So you've got to think ahead. Which, believe it or not, is just what the Government is doing.'

Seymour didn't believe it. In his experience, which was of the ministry responsible for the police, the Home Office, ministers didn't think ahead. They just improvised on the spot, after the event, when it was already too late.

'It's this new bloke,' said the Admiral. 'Did you know we've got a new bloke at the Admiralty?'

Seymour didn't. In the East End Naval affairs did not loom large.

'Yes. There's been a switch around and we've got a new bloke. Churchill, his name is. Doesn't know anything about the Navy, of course. Been a soldier. Well, there's nothing wrong with that, but it doesn't get you far when you're managing ships. But this new bloke seems actually to have a few ideas, and some of them are not totally daft. For instance, he intends to switch the whole Navy from coal to oil. Fisher's idea, of course, but a good one.'

He looked expectantly at Seymour. Seymour could see this was significant but for the life of him he couldn't see why. Something to do with fuel, obviously. What made ships go. Until now he had not, actually, ever thought about this. If anything, he was still living mentally in the world of sail. Of course, he knew, vaguely, that sail was being superseded by steam. That must be the coal. And now, apparently, coal was being superseded in its turn by oil.

'Hmm,' he said, trying to sound impressed. 'Important, I imagine.'

'It is!' said the Admiral enthusiastically. 'You can see at once the implications it has for us!'

'Oh, yes!' said Seymour. 'Oh, yes.'

'Take refuelling times, for instance. With oil, all you've got to do is stick a pipe in and then pump. With coal, you've got to have dozens of people shovelling. Takes hours. The switch from coal to oil will cut refuelling times – and, therefore, turn-round times – by four-fifths!'

'Amazing!' said Seymour.

'Oh, it's going to be. And that's not the end of it. It will revolutionize the way we do things. But we've got to get on with it. Otherwise, the Germans will do it first. In fact, they probably *have* done it first! But – and this is where I really do take my hat off to the Government – in one respect we're ahead of them.'

'We are? Oh, good!'

The Admiral paused dramatically, then lowered his voice.

'We've got the oil,' he said.

'Got the –?'

'Yes. Stitched it up. Bought the Anglo-Persian Oil Company. Guaranteed the Navy's oil supplies for years.'

'Well, that's splendid!'

'And I don't need to tell you the difference that will make!'

'No, indeed!'

'And this is where Lockhart comes in.'

'Lockhart?' said Seymour with a start.

'Yes. You see, until this Anglo-Persian deal, we hadn't been sure where our oil was going to come from. We'd been thinking about it, of course. *I'd* been thinking about it. Thought about little else from the moment I knew the switch was in the offing. I'd been making forward contracts, building storage tanks, trying to find suppliers – and this, of course, is where Lockhart came in.'

'Lockhart?'

'Yes. With his contacts. All through the Middle East. Especially with the Arabs. Now, of course, he wasn't dealing directly with the Persians. But he had plenty of ways of dealing with them indirectly, and I found him invaluable.

'It had to be done quietly, you see. We were ahead of the game, and we didn't want to let on to anyone else. And that was especially important to me, down in the Med, with the Turks at one end, and the Germans in cahoots with them, letting them have warships.

'Of course, once the Anglo-Persian oil started coming through, we'd be all right. But until then we were scratching around for oil. And that was where Lockhart came in with his connections. As I said, he was invaluable.

'So when I heard – and this was two years ago, remember, when things were still in the balance, and before the Anglo-Persian oil had really started flowing – that Lockhart had been murdered, I thought: hello, someone's putting their finger in my pie! And I didn't like it. By then I looked on Lockhart as one of my people. If someone was out to get him, I was out to get them.

'So I went to the Foreign Office and said, "This is an Englishman. More than that, he's one of my people, so you've got to do something." Did they do anything? Did they hell! They just faffed around, pushing papers in all directions, referring it here, taking it up there. I think they hoped I would go away. But once I've got my teeth into something, I don't let go and I'd got my teeth into this. And I still have. I want to know who killed Lockhart. And that, I hope, is what you're eventually going to tell me.'

Seymour, in fact, had come across the Admiral's 'new bloke' previously. Before he had been switched to the Admiralty, Churchill had been Minister at the Home Office, in charge, among other things, of the police. And there he had put Scotland Yard's back up in no small way.

This had been over the famous – or notorious – 'Siege of Sidney Street', as the newspapers had called it. A small armed gang had tried to break into an East End jeweller's. Surprised in the act, they had shot three policemen and then, hotly pursued, had taken refuge in a house in Sidney

Street where they had been trapped. Shooting was rare in London's underworld and the case had made big headlines in the press. And where there were big headlines, there were usually, in Seymour's experience, shortly afterwards big politicians. Churchill had interested himself personally in the case and had turned up on the spot; to be photographed for the newspapers, some said unkindly.

Worse, though, in the eyes of the police, he had called in the Army. He had even gone to the lengths of summoning up a field gun – this, for a relatively small incident, in the crowded streets of the East End, when the criminals were already trapped! Seymour was not alone in thinking that this tended towards overkill. However, it had gone down well in the newspapers.

Sidney Street was in Seymour's patch and what made it even more irritating was that he had had an inkling of what was planned and had been quietly taking steps to thwart it. In his view he could have wrapped the whole thing up without the need for heavy artillery.

He had been especially anxious to do this because the area had a considerable immigrant population. Indeed, some of the gang had immigrant connections. Seymour had been eager to avoid wider repercussions in the local community. But, of course, the immigrant connection, and also a later discovery that some of them had been anarchists, was too much for the press to resist and it had had a field day. Which had not helped either with solving the crime or in relations with the community.

So, yes, Seymour had heard of Churchill; and privately thought him a trigger-happy Boy Scout with an ego larger than one of the Admiral's battleships, a man who, if there was not a war already going on, was just the person to start one.

Seymour had arranged to meet Chantale at the Pension Francia, where, unknowingly, he had previously booked a room, and he went there now with a certain amount of apprehension. Chantale met him with a smile, however, and took him up to their room almost with pride. It was certainly very clean and respectable. But, then, so, it appeared, was the hotel as a whole; not at all what Seymour's fears had projected after what the midshipman had said.

It was clearly a place used by the Navy. There were sturdy, weather-beaten men standing around, often with sturdy weather-beaten ladies. These were not exactly houris, however, but motherly figures, homely rather than alluring, and talking practically about dhobi-men and dhobi-marks and when houses were going to come up. There were, it is true, a few ladies who might have been houris, slim, elegant but dressed just a little too nonchalantly, and with an over-easy familiarity of address. But it took all sorts to make a world, Seymour reflected, and, probably, especially the Naval world.

One thing was definitely clear: there was no colour-bar in that world. The ladies came from all parts of the globe. There were Chinese, Indians, South Americans and Caribbeans. And they seemed to mix on terms on which, possibly, in the wardroom they might not mix.

Their room had a little balcony and they went out on to it. There were some people standing below it, talking. One of the voices sounded familiar.

'Yes, I can let you have some calico. There's a new roll just come in. It's slightly spoiled at one end where the sea water got to it but it's nothing. You can cut if off, or I'll cut it off for you, and the rest is as good as new. Or if you like, I'll leave it on and adjust the price accordingly. It depends what you want it for. It's only slightly spoiled so if you're not too bothered, you can have that bit too and have it cheap. Only the thing is, see, I won't be able to let you have it for a day or two. It's got to be signed off, and that could take a bit of time just at the moment. The boss says things have got to be just so. Just at the moment.'

And now Seymour knew whose the voice was. It was that of the man he had heard in the guardroom, the one whom the midshipman had been so mercilessly teasing, Ferry.

'You interested? I'll make a note of it if you are. In my mind. No, I'm not going to write it down. These things are best not written down. But I'll remember it. You can count on it, right? Price? I'll have to come back to you on that, but say five quid. No, not for the roll. For the yard. A lot? No, no, no, no! It's dirt cheap. This is best quality calico. Straight from Pompey. You won't find this sort of thing in the souk and you won't find it at this sort of price anywhere. You need to think about it? Well, don't think too long or you'll lose the chance. There's others after it. Best quality, this is, apart from the little bit that's spoiled. And there's plenty of people interested. I can keep it for a day or two, but only for a day or two. Say Friday. By then the bastard will have gone.'

The people beneath moved away.

'You don't need some calico, do you?' said Seymour.

'Calico?' Chantale stared at him. 'What would I want that for?'

'Oh, I don't know. Make a sail, perhaps? Is that the sort of thing they make sails from?'

'Why would I want to make a sail?'

'Maybe it had better be something else. Can you think of another material?'

'Gingham?'

'I don't think they're likely to have much of that in ships' stores. Perhaps you'd better put it more generally? "Any chance of getting some material cheap?" That sort of thing.'

'And who am I supposed to ask?'

'Don't go to him directly. Ask around. I have a feeling that the women here will know.'

Señora Lockhart's house was a large white one with little balconies in front of the upper windows, over which bright red geraniums trailed in abundance. When he rang the bell an Arab servant girl came to the door.

She showed them into a dark entrance hall at the other end of which an open door led into a small inner court-yard, in the middle of which a fountain was playing. At one corner a broad flight of steps led up to a kind of half-verandah, on which were strewn some large leather cushions. They were shown up to these and the servant girl brought them glasses of lemonade.

Chantale looked around her in surprise.

'It's just like an Arab house!' she said.

A moment later Señora Lockhart came on to the veran-dah and they saw why. She was an Arab herself; small, almost bird-like, with slender arms and feet, middle-aged, and with a sharp Arab face and bright intelligent eyes.

She advanced on Seymour and held out her hand.

'Mr Seymour?' she said in English. 'I am very pleased to see you. My friend, 'Attersley, told me that you might be coming.'

'And this is Mademoiselle de Lissac,' said Seymour.

The sharp brown eyes took in Chantale. 'From Morocco?'

'Tangier.'

'I know it well.'

'You know my mother, perhaps? Madame de Lissac?'

She thought. 'I think I've heard of her in some connec-tion. But, no, I don't think I've actually met her. It's been a while since I was last in Tangier. And your father: he is French, of course.'

Seymour felt that the sharp eyes had grasped at once much of Chantale's situation: just possibly because she had known it for herself.

'Yes,' said Chantale. 'But he is dead.'

'Ah, *pardon*!' She took Chantale's hand in both of hers and pressed it sympathetically. '*Un militaire?*'

'*Oui.*'

'I am so sorry!'

Back in English. Like many people who were familiar

with several languages, like Seymour himself, she moved readily from one to another.

'You are welcome,' she said softly to Chantale.

They sat down on the leather cushions.

'I don't know if Señor Hattersley explained,' said Seymour, 'but I am a policeman from England. And I have come to Spain – and to Gibraltar – to find out what I can about how your husband died.'

'Yes, he did tell me that,' said Señora Lockhart. 'But what he did not tell me, was why anyone in England should be interested in how my husband died.'

'Because he was English, Señora.'

She laughed. 'He always denied that. He said he was Scottish and that was quite different.'

'Perhaps I should have said British.'

'He would admit to that on occasions,' she conceded. 'Especially,' she added drily, 'when it suited him.'

'So I have heard. And I think it is probably partly because of that that people in England are interested in what happened to him.'

'David 'Attersley again?'

'Admiral Comber, rather.'

'Ah, yes. The Admiral.'

'Does it surprise you that the Admiral should be interested?'

'I knew about what Lockhart was doing for him, if that's what you are asking.'

'The Admiral thinks that could be something to do with his death.'

Señora Lockhart did not respond.

'There are so many things,' she said, after a moment, 'that could be to do with his death.'

'Yes. Public as well as private.'

'Public?'

'What he was doing for the Admiral, for example. But also, perhaps, what he was doing for the Catalonians. Or, for that matter, the anarchists. But also private.'

'Such as?'

'I was hoping you might be able to tell me that.'

The Señora did not reply for quite a long time. Then she said, 'I don't know that I can tell you that. Or would want to. These things are, as you say, private. And perhaps it is best if they remain so.'

'I have no wish to pry. But if they are at all to do with his death, is it not right that they should be told?'

'I do not know. Is there to be no end to the damage?'

She was silent again for a moment and then she said, 'You spoke of rightness, and you think of truth and of justice. But you think of it in a cold English way. No, I am not fair. I do not know you, nor the way you think. And 'Attersley – well, whatever 'Attersley may be, he is not cold. He is hot that justice should be done to my husband. But there are different sorts of justice. There is the cold, English sort but there is also a justice to feeling, and I do not know what, in the end, is the sort of justice my husband would have wanted. He was English, of course: but he was also –' she smiled secretly to herself – 'a man of feeling. "Why," I said to him once, "you are almost an Arab!" "I am, I am," he said. "And that is why you married me."

'And it was true. When I first knew him he seemed to me so cold, so stiff, so English. Always calculating. That was how he struck me. Always in control of himself so that he could control others. So unfeeling. But then, suddenly, the feeling would break out, quite unexpectedly, over all sorts of things, trifles, even, and sweep you away. and I loved him for it. Do you understand me, Mademoiselle?' she appealed to Chantale.

'I think I do.'

'An Arab woman is passionate and responds to passion. Is that not so?'

Chantale laughed. 'I think it is. But perhaps it is so of all women. But I am sure you are right that we do not always read our men. Sometimes we expect passion and it is not there.'

77

Seymour was not entirely happy about this.

'And sometimes we don't expect it but then it suddenly erupts and we are bowled over by it!'

'Exactly so!' said Señora Lockhart, delighted. '"Bowled over". That is a good way of putting it. He would have liked that. But that, you see, was how he was. About all sorts of things. The Catalonians! The Algerians! The Moroccans – to make war on them seemed a terrible thing to him, and to use the Catalonians to do it –'

'Señora,' said Seymour, 'forgive me, but you are slipping away. These things are public, but were there not private things, too, that engaged his feelings?'

She gave him a long, appraising look, as if he needed to be weighed up before she would tell him anything.

'He was a man of feeling, as I have told you. He felt strongly, yes. And sometimes he felt strongly about people.'

'Particular people?'

'People are always particular.'

'You are trying to slip away again, Señora.'

She laughed.

'Perhaps I am,' she admitted. 'But, you see, sometimes with his strong, erratic feelings he hurt people. Unjustly. And why should I add to that injustice? There is, as I said before, a justice to feeling as there is to fact.'

'Can you help me a little more with that justice to feeling?'

'I don't think I can. This is not something that can be approached in a cold, objective, English way. It is, I think, something you have to be an Arab to understand.'

As they were going down the steps into the courtyard, they met a man coming up.

'Why, Abou!' cried Señora Lockhart. 'Where have you been? I expected you an hour ago! This is my brother,' she said to Seymour and Chantale, 'and he is always late.'

'I am sorry, I am sorry. They caught me just as I was leaving the office and said that something had come through about that spoiled cargo.'

'Abou has been helping me on the business side,' said Señora Lockhart, 'ever since –'

'You don't need help, really,' said Abou.

'Not now, perhaps,' said Señora Lockhart, 'but at first –'

'I couldn't leave you on your own,' said Abou. 'It wouldn't be right. What is a brother for?'

'He had come over from Algiers just before,' said Señora Lockhart. 'Just for a short visit. But then he decided to stay.'

'I couldn't do anything else, could I? Not with you left alone.'

'Ah, family, family!' said Señora Lockhart. She put her hand on her brother's arm. 'But I am glad you did stay,' she said softly.

'And now she wants to get rid of me!'

'No, no!' laughed Señora Lockhart.

'Send me back to Algiers.'

'You are needed there, too. And, anyway, you suggested it. We agreed to divide the management,' she said to Seymour. 'He would look after the marine side while I concentrated on the financial side.'

'It is better like that,' Abou said. 'It is harder to accept a woman in Algeria than it is in Spain.'

'This is Señor Seymour,' said Señora Lockhart. 'He is a policeman. And he has come out from London to look into Lockhart's death.'

'Really?' said Abou, surprised. 'From England?' Then he laughed. 'England doesn't think the Spanish police are up to it?'

'No, no –'

'Nor do I,' he said drily. 'Well, I hope you get somewhere. It hangs over us, it hangs over us. Among my people these things cannot be left. They have to be resolved, one way or another. I wish you success.'

79

He shook hands and started off up the stairs. As he did so he appeared to register, for the first time, Chantale's presence.

'Señora! I beg your pardon.'

He gave her a little, quick, formal, Spanish bow.

'Mademoiselle de Lissac,' said Señora Lockhart.

'A thousand pardons, Mademoiselle.'

He seemed to see her properly for the first time. And then there was the start back that Seymour had become used to.

'Mademoiselle . . .' he said, slightly puzzled, looking at his sister.

'Mademoiselle de Lissac is from Tangier,' she said.

'Ah! You are, perhaps,' he said hesitantly, 'a friend of Señor Lockhart's?'

'No,' said Señora Lockhart firmly.

Chapter Six

To his surprise, that afternoon he saw someone he recognized at the Pension Francia. It was Nina, the anarchist schoolteacher. At first he thought he must be mistaken. Wasn't this term-time and wouldn't Nina have been at her school on the other side of Spain? But, no, it definitely was her, and Chantale confirmed it.

She was with an older lady and they were standing at the other end of the corridor. A moment later they disappeared into a room.

He hesitated, and then went along the corridor. The door of the room was open and he looked inside. It led into a small sitting room, one reserved for the use of guests. He hesitated again and then went in.

Nina and the older lady were sitting together on a sofa. They obviously knew each other well: but there was clearly a tension between them. It was almost as if Nina was glowering at the other woman. Certainly the relationship seemed prickly, but then, thought Seymour, that could well have been true of most of Nina's relationships with people.

She looked up in surprise when he and Chantale came in and gave them, if not, perhaps, a welcoming smile, at least an indication of recognition.

'Señor –'

'Señorita!'

'And Señora!' said Nina, looking at Chantale. Wrongly, because Chantale was still a señorita; unless being slightly older than Nina entitled her to extra respect.

She turned to the woman sitting beside her. 'These are friends who came to the school.'

'Ah, yes?' said the lady.

'And this is my mother.'

'Your mother?' said Seymour, slightly surprised; slightly surprised, in fact, that Nina had a mother, or was prepared to acknowledge one. But if she was her mother that probably accounted for the tension.

'*Si*. I am visiting her.'

'I expect you don't often get a chance to see your daughter, Señora, with her living in Barcelona.'

'Once or twice a year,' said the woman. 'Which is not nearly enough.'

Nina gave a sort of petulant shrug.

'And you, Señor?' said the mother. 'You are not from Spain, I think?'

'From England,' said Nina. 'He is a policeman. He has come out to investigate Lockhart's death.'

Her mother seemed to flinch.

'My mother knew Lockhart,' said Nina.

'Did you, Señora?'

'Yes,' she said, unwillingly. 'Yes. I have known him for a long time. Ever since he came over to Spain, in fact. From when he first came to Gibraltar.'

'He was very good to my mother when my father died,' said Nina.

'Yes,' said her mother; again, almost reluctantly.

'My father was in the Spanish Customs Office. Here in Gibraltar. And Lockhart and he were great friends.'

'Yes,' said her mother.

'It was hard for her when my father died. Especially at first, before the pension came through. He paid the rent, and other things.'

'Yes,' said her mother. 'He was always generous in that way.'

'And took an interest in me as I grew up. He was a sort of – godfather? Is that the right word?'

82

'Yes, I think so,' said Seymour.

'He was the only one who was kind to me at the convent.'

'Nina!' protested her mother. 'That is not true!'

'It is!' said Nina fiercely. 'The nuns were horrible old women, and I hated them!'

'Nina –'

'Well, it's true!' Nina insisted. 'They used to beat me.'

'Nina –'

'They liked it, I think.'

'Nina, that is *not* true. They may have seemed hard, *been* a little hard to you, but you were unruly and perhaps sometimes you deserved it.'

'I always said that when I grew up, I would fight them,' said Nina. 'And I have.'

Her mother gave a little, despairing shrug. 'It is wrong to bear hatred in your heart, Nina.'

'It is better to bear hatred than to let them do what they want with you!'

Her mother shrugged again, but looked sad. This was probably familiar ground to her.

'And, perhaps *your* school, as opposed to their school, was a way of fighting back?' suggested Seymour.

Nina beamed.

'That is precisely so!' she said.

'And was that why Lockhart helped the school? Gave money to start it and support it?'

'Yes, for me, yes. And because he wanted children to be free.'

'He should have wanted them to be good,' said her mother.

'Good, yes, perhaps,' said Nina. 'But free first!'

'Anyway, it was right that he came to see you at the convent,' said her mother.

'It was, yes. Otherwise I think I might have died.'

'Nina –'

'Killed myself.'

'Nina, Nina! That would be a sin!'

'I wanted to sometimes. There was no escape. Either from them or from the place. I felt suffocated. For years I seemed to live in endless darkness.'

'It was, perhaps, a mistake to send you to that one,' her mother admitted. 'I should have chosen another. Where it was less harsh. But at the time –'

Nina put her hand on her mother's arm.

'I understand that,' she said, with awkward tenderness, 'but –'

'I am glad that at any rate he came to see you.'

'He was a candle in the darkness,' said Nina. 'The only ray of light!'

Her mother shook her head.

'It was very good of him,' she said. 'But sometimes I wish he had not.'

Seymour went out early the next morning to sniff the sea. The smell was a different one from that of the murky waters of the East End docks; he never felt inclined to go down in the morning and sniff those! They were dirty and oily and acidic, the tang so strong some days as to make you retch. That was when the fog lay heavily over London, when the smells of the docks were reinforced by the fumes rising from the old, closed courts of the east, the working, end of the city, where small workshops fed smoke into the thick, choking air that he had known from childhood.

Gibraltar was not like that. It opened out at once into the blue, glittering width of the bay and the air came in straight from the open sea. In front of him the long arm of the Old Mole curled round with just a few small boats this side of it. Behind him were the tall, thin buildings of the Old Town, with its narrow streets rising up the hill to the crenellations of the ancient Moorish castle. And, over to the side, stretching away into the far distance, were the peaks and crests of the mountains of Andalusia.

Everywhere there was warmth and light. The sun, only just becoming hot on his face, was burning the last early morning mists off the sea. The air, which later would become hot, and possibly unpleasantly so, still felt fresh in his face. He breathed deep.

Chantale would like this, he thought. He must bring her here tomorrow morning. She would enjoy the continuation of freshness and warmth, which would remind her of Tangier, and respond to the feeling of openness which came from the great bay opening up with the sea and escaping from the hills closing in behind.

And then a second thought struck him, the old, nagging doubt: could he ask her to exchange this – the sun and warmth and light – for the constricted, choking darkness of London's dockland? Was it fair? Was it right?

Seymour had come down to the sea front so early because he was reckoning to spend the whole day making his nominal inspection of the stores. With luck that would be enough to establish a reason for his being in Spain and divert attention from the real purpose of his inquiries.

He met McPhail, still the Duty Officer, at the guardroom and walked over with him to the stores.

'Are you finding the Francia to your taste, sir?' the midshipman said, with a knowing smile.

The reason for the knowing smile was soon apparent. Word had got round that Seymour had Chantale with him. As he went into the stores he heard the petty officer's voice at the far end. For a moment he was obscured by the shelving and Ferry did not see him.

'*And* he's brought his bird with him!'

'Well, what's wrong with that?' asked another voice. 'Wouldn't you do the same?'

'Yes, but he's on duty, like. How did he manage that? Fly bastard, isn't he? I wonder who's paying?'

'Not him, I don't suppose. What's she like?'

'A bit of all right. I wouldn't mind having a quiet evening walk along the Mole with her myself!'

'What would Bella say to that?'

'Bella would never know!'

'How do you know he's brought his bird with him?' challenged another voice.

'I saw them at the Francia.'

'Well, that's the place to stay, isn't it, if you're like that.'

'Your fame precedes you, sir,' murmured McPhail.

'Just as it should!' said the Admiral, over a drink at lunch in the wardroom. He gave Seymour one of the knowing looks. 'Got your girlfriend with you, I gather?'

It didn't take long for the news to get around, thought Seymour. He began to wonder if it had, after all, been such a good idea to bring Chantale over. Suppose word got back to London?

'Ah, I think you're thinking of Mademoiselle de Lissac,' he said. 'She's assisting me at this end.'

'Good-looker, I hear. You obviously know how to pick them.'

'Purely for their Intelligence skills,' said Seymour, hoping that that would get around, too.

'Are we going to have a chance of seeing your assistant, sir?' asked McPhail, as he was taking Seymour back to the stores, after lunch.

'Maybe. But she's busy pursuing her own line of inquiries.'

'That would be, I understand,' said McPhail hesitantly, 'in the way of Intelligence?'

'Yes. She's Intelligence, I'm policing. I think there's a question of broadening the inquiry.'

* * *

86

'Jesus!' he heard Ferry say. 'They've brought bloody Intelligence in as well?'

'Here, I don't like the sound of this. It sounds a bit bigger than we thought.'

'What the hell's Intelligence got to do with this?' said Ferry's worried voice. 'Just how deep are they going?'

Not very deep, if Seymour's own inquiries were anything to go by. He was never at his best on this kind of thing. His mind glazed over as he went from one section of the stores to another, and seized up completely when he was confronted with that mysterious thing, 'the Books'.

'He don't look happy!' he heard someone whisper to Ferry.

'Jesus!'

Even McPhail was impressed.

'Are you on to something, sir?'

'Just a few questions in my mind, that's all.'

Like, when could he decently stop for a drink?

'You've got to remember, sir,' said McPhail, already beginning to see a need to come to the defence of his men, 'that the Navy is not quite the same as a shore establishment. We've got our own ways of doing things.'

'Yes, I see that,' said Seymour.

It was a neutral, fobbing-off remark, and he intended nothing by it; but it had a disconcerting effect in the stores generally.

'You're going to have to smarten up your act, Ferry,' Seymour heard the midshipman say.

A little later Ferry approached Seymour.

'Of course, things may not be quite shipshape, sir. The fact is, there's a lot of pilfering when you're on shore. These bloody natives!'

'The Gibraltarese?'

'That's right. Bloody get their hands on anything. You've got to watch them like a hawk. And that, though I say it myself, sir, is what I do. Keep my eyes skinned all the time. Even come here after dark occasionally, when I'm not really on watch. Just to see nobody's breaking in. Because that's what they do, sir, all the time. Unless you're keeping a good lookout.'

'It's just as well you do, Mr Ferry.'

'Ah, it is, sir. It is. Things go missing.'

'I'm sure they do.'

Again, he meant nothing by it. But it didn't seem to assuage the petty officer's uneasiness at all.

Midshipman McPhail's thoughts, however, were turning, with the buoyancy of youth, away from the temporary tribulations of the store room and to more permanent interests.

'I was wondering, sir,' he said, as they walked away at the end of the afternoon, 'whether your assistant would come to join us in the bar this evening?'

'I'm sure she would like to. This evening, alas, she has an engagement already.'

'A pity, sir. Perhaps some other time? We're all rather eager to make her acquaintance, sir.'

I'll bet you are, thought Seymour.

'She *is* rather striking, sir.'

'Yes, I think so, too.'

Perhaps it was time for a shot across the bows.

'She is, of course, married.'

'She is?' said McPhail, downcast.

'Or very nearly,' a slightly optimistic definition of the truth compelled him to add.

'Knot not yet tied?' said McPhail, cheering up.

'Practically,' said Seymour.

'Oh, well,' said the midshipman, 'it would be nice to see her at the bar anyway.'

He seemed, however, to be weighing something in his mind.

'She's – she's not an accountant, is she?' he said hesitantly.

'Good Lord, no! Nothing like that! She's quite normal.'

The next day was the King's birthday: a fact which had somehow escaped Seymour's notice. But the Royal Birthday, Hattersley assured him, played big in Gibraltar. The Navy would dress ships, fire salutes, supply a band, march in procession, and hold a tea party for His Majesty's loyal subjects. Everyone, but everyone, said Hattersley firmly, would be there, and he clearly took it for granted that Seymour would be, too.

Seymour was not so sure. True it could give him an opportunity to talk to members of Gibraltar's trading community – Leila Lockhart would be there, for instance – which he quite wanted to do. They would all have known Lockhart and might be able to give him some useful information. On the other hand, however, he had arranged to spend a further, last, day in the stores and thought that by the time he had finished that, the last thing he would want to do would be to attend what was clearly going to be a heavily Imperial Occasion. No, if the day was to be cut short, he could put it to far better use. He and Chantale could –

But then he received an official invitation from the Admiral at the bottom of which was a pencilled request that Seymour should join him for a drink afterwards, together with a further request, underlined, that he should bring his Assistant (Intelligence) with him.

A roped-off enclosure on an immaculate green lawn overlooking the sea; a gigantic, seven-foot-high hat striding around, which, on inspection, had the Governor under it; ladies in feathers and ensembles which had been the glory of the London Season several seasons ago; Naval uniforms heavy with golden braid; besuited gentlemen, some of them ruddy-faced from England, others darker and browner and from a variety of places around the Mediterranean; a few unquestionably Spanish but keeping quiet about it – this was what struck Seymour when he arrived at the tea party.

There were quite a few children: cleaned up for the occasion but already sticky from the sugared cakes unwisely left unguarded on a table. And rather fewer presentable women in their early twenties, thought Seymour, with the usual male eye; although quite a lot of less presentable women in the over-twenties. Among them was Chantale, not, in her view, satisfactorily dressed, but surrounded by a gaggle – or should it be goggle? – of Naval admirers.

Seymour moved among the suits.

'Sam Lockhart? Knew him well. Bad business, that. But that's what you get, mixing with the Spaniards.'

'And the Arabs,' put in his neighbour.

'And the Arabs, of course,' conceded the first businessman.

'Of course, that's where his business was,' said the second.

'And look where it got him!'

Not a lot there, thought Seymour, and moved on.

'Problems with the Spanish Customs? Who hasn't had problems with them? But Sam had it more worked out than most of us. A little bit of this, I fancy!' – rubbing imaginary banknotes between the fingers.

A uniform to outshine even the Navy, which could only belong to a Spanish Customs official.

'Señor Lockhart? We miss him. A reasonable man – and there are not, Señor, that many reasonable men in a place like this! Sympathies?' A shrug. 'We all have sympathies. But we learn to keep them quiet. Now Señor Lockhart never could do that. If it was not the anarchists it was the Arabs. Catalonians? There are no Catalonian Nationalists in Spain.'

His companion, also dripping with gilt:

'Tragic Week? The name says it all. That's what it was. A tragic week for Spain, not just for those unfortunates caught up in it. And why Señor Lockhart got caught up in it, I cannot think. But oh, yes, I can. He was a man, Señor, in whom feeling outran discretion. You know? He would see someone being robbed and then, instead of staying sensibly out of it, would rush to intervene. Killed? Frankly, Señor, I'm surprised he stayed alive so long! Especially in Barcelona. Especially in Tragic Week.' The Customs official laid his finger alongside his nose. 'You know, Señor. A week for paying off scores. Among so many, who would notice a few more? And that, maybe, was how it was with Señor Lockhart.'

More useful, perhaps, to talk to the women.

'Ah, yes, Señor, that is Señora Lockhart. So sad! You have heard, yes? A wronged woman.'

'Wronged?'

'Well, yes, Señor. Señor Lockhart, although a good man, a very good man, and especially a good man to have a private tête-à-tête with in a carriage on a dark evening, was, nevertheless, a little bit forward. In too much of a hurry, yes? Spanish women like to hold back, to tease. But the Señor would accept only a little teasing, and then he would want to proceed to – well, you know, Señor! You know what men are! Are you like that, Señor?' – taking his arm. 'Señor Lockhart?' – pouting. 'Why are we talking about him? Well, if you insist ... The fact is, Señor, he did not confine his attentions to unmarried ladies. Well, that is all right. Married ladies can tease, too. But sometimes men – husbands especially – do not understand. And that, I think, is perhaps what happened in Señor Lockhart's case. A wronged husband. No, I cannot think of one in particular. There were –' archly – 'so many!'

An English lady was more specific.

'Sam?' – laughing. 'A right one he was! A wife in every port – and there were a lot of ports in his business! It was only a question of time before someone caught up with him. And, if you really want to know what I think, I think that's exactly what happened. They say there was a woman in Barcelona, the wife of a high-up official. And that he seized the opportunity of Tragic Week to settle the score!'

It might be worth looking into, thought Seymour. But, on the whole, he thought it was more likely to be romantic rather than real. Jealousy was supposed to be a big thing in Spain. He himself did not go in for jealousy.

He looked around to see how Chantale was getting on and if she was in need of any assistance. She didn't seem to be, however. In fact, she seemed to be rather enjoying herself. Seymour was not a man to feel jealous, but . . . Well, on second thoughts, maybe he *was* a man to feel jealous. All those over-excited and, possibly, in her eyes at least, glamorous Naval officers clamouring round her. In a moment, he thought, he would go over and extricate her. Use their drink with the Admiral as pretext.

There *was* the Admiral. Talking to Leila Lockhart. They seemed to be deep in a serious conversation, not chattering idly. He half thought of going over but decided not to. He shouldn't interrupt them.

Standing not far away, on duty, so to speak, was Leila's brother, alone. Seymour had seen him earlier talking to one or two of the businessmen, only to the men not to any of the women. But now he wasn't talking to anybody, he was just standing there looking bored.

He noticed Seymour and came across to him.

'Señor . . .? I am sorry, I have forgotten your name, but I do remember – you came to visit us, yes?'

'Yes. Seymour.'

'And your lady,' He glanced round. 'She is not here?'

'Over there.'

'Ah, yes.

He saw the knot of sailors.

'You do not mind?' he said.

'I think she can look after herself.'

'Yes, that is what Leila says. She can look after herself, she says. That is what women here say. But I do not think they are right. They are sometimes foolish. They let things go further than they should, and then it gets out of hand.'

He put up an apologetic hand. 'I am not, of course, saying that your lady . . . But . . . It is different here. Your society and my society are different. I would never let my wife . . . But it is different here, yes. Leila is always saying that to me. "Things do not mean the same," she says. "What looks to you like an immodest invitation means nothing of the sort over here. It is just social warmth." Well, I take her word for it. But I find it strange.'

When Seymour got back to Barcelona he found a message from Manuel waiting for him. It said that Manuel would like to see him, so he went round to the café right away. It was late in the afternoon and the café was almost empty. It would fill up later when people on their way home from work started dropping in for their aperitif. Most of the staff came on duty then, too, and the only person there now was Dolores, wiping the tables.

'Manuel?'

She disappeared inside. A moment later she came back.

'He's been having his siesta,' she said. 'He's just getting up. He says to give you a beer.'

She put a beer on the table in front of him.

'Where have you been?' she said. 'The *cabezudos* have been wondering. They think you might have gone back to England.'

'I've been to Gibraltar.'

'Ah? Where Mr Lockhart came from?'

'That's right. I've been talking to Mrs Lockhart.'

'*Mrs* Lockhart,' said Dolores bitterly. 'Well, that must have been a pleasure.'

Seymour said nothing.

'You might have been talking to me,' said Dolores wistfully.

'It wouldn't have made any difference,' said Seymour. 'Lockhart would still have been dead.'

'How do you know?' said Dolores. She bent over a table and rubbed it hard. 'I would have looked after him better.'

Manuel came out and sat down beside him. Dolores scuttled away to the other side of the café. A moment later she went outside and began to wipe the tables there.

'It has not been easy,' said Manuel. 'I have had to spend money.'

'How much?'

'Sixty.' He put his hand on Seymour. 'Don't give it me now. We may have to spend more. Have you some cash with you? Good. We may need it when we get there. The sixty has all gone on just getting them ready to listen.'

'I understand.'

Manuel got up from the table.

'We'll go now,' he said, 'if that's all right. I don't want to leave it too long or else they'll change their mind. And that will mean more money.'

When they got to the prison, he didn't go to the main entrance but to a little door round the side.

'Ah, there you are!' said the man who opened it.

They went in.

'That'll be twenty.'

'You've had twenty.'

The man shrugged. 'This was to square things inside.'

Manuel gave the man another twenty.

He led them along a corridor and then up some stone steps, and then along another corridor to a staircase. They went up the staircase to another long, bare corridor with doors along it. He stopped outside one of these.

'You can have twenty minutes,' he said.

He unlocked the door and they all three went in.

'Right,' said the man, who appeared to be a warder of some kind, 'you've got visitors!'

It was pitch black and Seymour couldn't see anything. He sensed people moving, however.

'Just watch it!' warned the warder. 'I don't want any trouble.'

There was a window, high up and barred off, but what Seymour wanted now was as much ventilation as it was light.

'I'll leave you,' said the warder. 'Remember, no trouble!' he warned.

'I'll stay with you,' said Manuel.

'Thanks.'

He might need the Spaniard to interpret if they got deep into Catalan.

'Has he got any fags?' asked someone.

'I might have,' said Manuel, who had come prepared.

He handed round cigarettes and soon to the stench of sweaty, unwashed bodies was added the acrid fumes of cheap cigarettes.

'I want to ask about someone,' said Seymour.

'Okay, ask.'

'An Englishman. His name was Lockhart.'

No one said anything.

'He was killed. Here. In the prison.'

'It happens,' said someone.

'How can it happen?'

There was a little laugh.

'Why do you want to know?' said someone.

'The father is asking,' said Manuel.

'The father?'

'The Englishman's father.'

'He shouldn't have let his son come here.'

'His son was killed during Tragic Week,' said Seymour.

'So were a lot of others.'

'This one was killed *after* they had put him in prison.'

There was another silence.

'He was a friend of the Catalonians,' said Manuel.

95

'And of the anarchists,' said Seymour. Then he wondered if that was wise.

'Lockhart?' a voice questioned.

'*Si.*'

'He was a friend of Arabs, too.'

'He seems to have been a friend of everybody!' said a voice caustically.

'But not of the authorities,' said Seymour.

There was another silence.

'Got any more fags?'

'Here!' said Manuel.

'How can a man die when he is in prison?' asked Seymour.

'Accident,' said someone. 'On his way along the corridor. Or in his cell.'

'The warders?'

'Perhaps.'

'They might let someone in,' said another voice. 'If they were told to.'

'The Englishman was poisoned,' said someone. He thought it may have been the Arab.

'He was,' said Seymour. 'How could that happen?'

'Easy. Get someone to poison the food.'

'The warders?'

'It would have to be, wouldn't it? If it was in the kitchens, *we'd* have been poisoned, too, wouldn't we?'

'So between the kitchen and the cell?'

No one replied.

'Do you always have the same warder?'

'One on during the day, the other on during the night.'

'The man who brought us?'

'Not him, no. Two others.'

'It would have been the last meal,' said someone. 'He was found dead in the morning.'

'And who brings the last meal?'

'The night warder.'

'Enrico.'

There was a sudden hammering on the door.

'One minute!'

'Señor,' said someone urgently, 'was this man truly a friend of Catalonia?'

'He was out on the streets in Tragic Week so that he could tell the world what he saw.'

'So the bastards made sure that he couldn't!'

The warder outside began to unlock the door.

Someone touched Seymour's arm.

'Señor,' he whispered, 'sometimes people bring food for those in the prison. It is forbidden but it is done. That is, perhaps, how the poison reached the Englishman.'

The warder came into the cell.

'Right!' he said. 'Time's up. If you're still alive.'

'It's only bastards like you, Diego, that we kill!'

Chapter Seven

Looking out from the balcony of his room he saw the Chief of Police standing in the plaza below.

'He's been hanging around,' Chantale said.

Seymour shrugged and then went back inside. But when he looked out again some time later the Chief was still there.

'Does it matter?' said Chantale.

'No. I'm just curious.'

The Chief marched across the square to the little anarchist school.

'I think I'll go down,' said Seymour.

The school had closed for the day but the two teachers were still busy in the playground doing something to one of the pieces of equipment. They didn't look up when the Chief arrived but he spoke to them and Nina went across.

Seymour got there in time to hear the exchange.

'So, Señora, you are still at work?'

'So, Chief, you are again not at work?'

'I *am* at work,' retorted the Chief with dignity. 'I am keeping an eye on things.'

'The glasses in the bar?'

'People,' said the Chief heavily. 'People who are up to something.'

'Well, you won't be keeping your eye on me, then,' said Nina, and turned to go.

'One moment, Señora!'

She stopped. '*Si?*'

'I have come to warn you.'

'Oh?'

'You are mixing with bad people, Señora.'

'Only when I talk to the police. Which isn't very often.'

The Chief breathed heavily. 'You will find yourself mixing with them more if you go on the way you are doing.'

'Oh? What way is that? Teaching our children?'

'How you teach your children is not my concern, Señora. Although it may be the Church's. It is what you do out of school that bothers me.'

'I do not break the law.'

'You do not treat it with respect.'

'It does not deserve respect. And nor, Chief, do you.'

The Chief reddened. 'I am giving you advice, Señora. Good advice. The next time it will not be advice. You will be back in jail. And this time there will be no one to bail you out.'

'Will you kill me, as you did him?'

'Señora –'

'I do not need your warnings,' said Nina scornfully.

'You do, Señora. And would do well to heed them. You mix with bad people.'

'Poor people,' said Nina. 'Not bad people.'

'Murderers.'

'What nonsense!' said Nina, beginning to turn away.

'We know who killed Ramon Mas.'

Nina stopped.

'No one killed him,' she said. 'He died when his boat sank.'

'Sank? Just like that? A fisherman's boat? One that was out on the water every night? No, no, Señora, boats like that do not sink. They sink only when somebody sinks them.'

'Why should anyone do that? He was a poor man, like us.'

'He knew too much. He was out on the water every night and he had seen. And he was going to tell.'

99

'He was an ordinary fisherman out with other fisher-men. What was there to tell? That he had seen the nets being pulled in, that he had seen fish leaping in the darkness.'

'Oh, more than that, Señora. More than that!'

'He was a poor fisherman and he died as other poor fishermen have done. Let him rest in peace. Do not draw him into your sick fantasies.'

'He was a poor fisherman, Señora, and needed money. Otherwise he was going to lose his boat. And he was not like your friends, Señora, he was not one of them. So why shouldn't he tell? The night before he died he met one of my men and they made an appointment. Someone must have heard them, for he did not keep it.'

'You think that because my friends are anarchists –'

'I think that because they are anarchists they do not fear God. Nor His justice. And I think you should have nothing to do with them. You are an innocent young girl without a father and your mind is full – well, you spoke of my sick fantasies. You should have regard to the beam in your own eye. And stay away from such men.'

Nina walked away. The Chief of Police stood for a moment watching her and then turned. He saw Seymour and beamed.

'Señor Seymour, it is good to have you back with us!'

'It is a pleasure to be back. Of course, I have not been away for very long.'

'At Gibraltar, did you say?'

Seymour hadn't said, but he guessed that this was a way of telling him that they knew.

'Gibraltar, yes.'

'I hope you had a fruitful time?'

'I did, yes.' And then, to rattle the Chief a little, 'More than I had expected.'

'Ah? Well, Señor, we have missed you. "I was just getting to know him," I said to Constanza. (That's my wife.) "Oh?" she said. "Well, that's very nice. Why don't you come home at a proper time one evening and get to know me? Instead of going out drinking."

'Well, there you are, Señor! That's a wife for you! She doesn't understand that a man needs a drink after a hard day's work. "A glass, yes; but a bottle?" she says. But it's only a bottle when I'm with friends. "Everyone's a friend if they buy you a drink!" she says. "We're talking business," I say. "There's obviously a lot of business," she says. Well, there is. That is why I am not home till late.'

'"I don't come home on the dot," I tell her, "because I am conscientious." "You don't come home on the dot," she says, "because you're a drunk."

'A drunk! What a thing for a wife to say to a husband! Does your wife say things like that, Señor? Ah, I was forgetting. Perhaps she is not your wife, the lady I met.'

He gave Seymour a rascally wink.

Then he looked around. 'Where is the beautiful Señora, by the way?'

'Out shopping.'

'Ah, shopping? Dangerous, dangerous. They run through the money as if it was water. A pity, Señor. I was hoping to take you both out for a drink.'

'Alas!' said Seymour. 'Another time, perhaps. But perhaps this time you will allow me to take *you* out for a drink?'

'Well . . .' said the Chief of Police.

He took Seymour to a little bar on Las Ramblas.

'I come here often,' he said.

'I'm sure.'

'But it is not as Constanza supposes. I come here to pursue my duties.'

'You do?'

'Yes. You know what they say about Las Ramblas? They say that on Las Ramblas you will meet everyone in

101

Barcelona that you know. Sitting here, they come to me. I don't go to them. I can keep an eye on what they're up to. See, for instance, who they talk to. And that suggests things. Things that might happen. Or things that have happened or might have happened. As with Señor Lockhart, for example.'

'Lockhart?'

'Yes. Whenever he came to Barcelona he would take a walk along Las Ramblas. and I would see him and see who he talked to. And I would see him talking to someone and say to myself: ah, so something's happening in that quarter, is it? And later something would happen. A bargain would be struck, a deal made. And I would have seen it coming. People say to me, "How do you know these things?" I know them because I have seen the beginnings of them. Here on Las Ramblas.

'Of course, Señor Lockhart used to talk to many people. It would be necessary to sift a bit. I would see him talking to someone and say to myself, "Ah, that is an old friend." Or perhaps I would see him talking to a pretty girl and say to myself, "Ah, there he goes again!" But in this way I learned a lot about Señor Lockhart.

'I would see him talking to the *cabezudos*, for example. He always talked to them, every time he came. He said they brought fun into the life of Barcelona. And that, perhaps, is true. But they also brought other things : disorder, misrule, subversion. The things that a Chief of Police has to keep his eye on. And I wondered why Señor Lockhart always talked to them.

'But the answer is clear, is it not? There was a side to Señor Lockhart that was sympathetic to them. It showed itself in other things; that crazy girl, for example, that you just saw me talking to. They tell me he used to give her money. For the school, he said. Well, I wonder about that. I, too, am keen on education. We would have sent our children to a good Catholic school. The one near St Mark's, for example. And when the Fathers come along, I put my hand in my pocket. But that is different from supporting a place like that. And I wonder if he really was supporting it, or whether – well, you know, Señor, some would see her as a pretty girl and maybe that's the way it was.

'She told me once she'd been to a decent Catholic school. A good convent school, she said. You would have thought, then, that she would have known better. But she said they were all nasty old bitches there. I told Constanza this, and she crossed herself, and said, "It takes one to know one."

'Well, I don't know about that. I always try to steer clear of religion when I'm talking to Constanza. But she's a difficult girl, that Nina, and a bit crazy. She's another one to steer clear of.

'But that school wasn't the only thing. There were other things, too. The Catalonians, for example, and the Arabs. He had time, too much time, for them all. And for any other cracked group of misfits. So I was not surprised when Tragic Week came along and he got mixed up in it. You could say I had seen it coming – here, on Las Ramblas. It was in the wind, in the air.'

The Chief gave a great sniff. 'You could say it was my job. To sniff the air and see when trouble's coming. And here on Las Ramblas is a good place to sniff it.'

He looked down into the bottom of his glass. It was empty.

'Another one?'

'Well . . .'

When they resumed, the Chief said, 'So when I sit here, with a glass in my hand, like this, I am not wasting my time. Despite what Constanza thinks. I am working. I am noticing things. And adding them up. I have watched Señor Lockhart from here many times. Watched what he does, who he talks to.

'And I think, Señor, that I have seen a process. It begins with a walk along Las Ramblas. Sampling the air, enjoying the fun. Talking to acquaintances, old friends. Acquaintances become old friends on Las Ramblas. And I have watched Señor Lockhart's friendships grow. They begin with a stop to watch, continue with a laugh, and then another laugh, develop into an exchange, into a conversation, and soon there is something more. There is a relationship.

'And that relationship leads on. One relationship leads to another. And in the end it led, in Señor Lockhart's case, to what happened during Tragic Week. That is what I think, Señor Seymour. It is like pitch. You touch it and it sticks to your fingers. But you also stick to it; and it draws you in. That is what I think happened to Señor Lockhart.

'And why I am telling you this is that I see in this also a risk for you. For you, too, Señor Seymour, have been touching pitch. I have watched you, too, and seen you talking to the *cabezudos*. And the beginning, perhaps, of a conversation?'

Afterwards, as he was walking back to the hotel, he wondered what the Chief of Police had been trying to tell him. Warning him, certainly; but about what? Not about talking to the *cabezudos*, surely. But who else was the 'pitch'? Again, surely not Nina. He had warned Nina, too. And there seemed to have been some grounds for that warning. Was that, what she had perhaps been mixed up in, the pitch?

While Seymour had been talking to the Chief, Chantale had gone for a walk of her own along Las Ramblas. On her way she had a strange encounter. She had noticed a man looking at her intently. Well, she was used to that and here, in Barcelona, she didn't mind it. In Tangier she would have felt uneasy and possibly a little apprehensive. Here, however, in some odd way, it added to the sense of freedom.

The man wavered and then suddenly came purposefully across to her.

104

'Señora,' he said apologetically, 'I would not ordinarily have approached you in such a way, in the absence of your husband. But I am in some difficulty and when I saw you, I thought, ah, yes, perhaps with her special knowledge she can help me.'

He spoke as if he had recognized her. And then, after a moment, she realized that she recognized him. It was Abou, Leila Lockhart's brother.

'Yes?' she said uncertainly.

'The fact is, I am in Barcelona for a special purpose.'

'Yes?' Still slightly uncertainly. If this was a sexual approach, it was a rather unusual one.

'I do not know the customs here,' he said.

'Well, I am not exactly an expert,' said Chantale, 'but if I can help –'

'I am going back to Algeria,' he said. 'Soon. Perhaps next week.'

'Yes?' she said, encouragingly.

But he seemed unable to say anything more. And then it come out with a rush.

'I want to arrange my marriage before I go.'

'Marriage?' said Chantale.

'Yes,' he said, and stopped again.

'Really?' said Chantale encouragingly. 'Marriage?'

'It is not easy here. In Algeria I would know what to do. I would make it known to my family and, if they approved, they would see to it. They would approach her family and between them they would settle it – the portion, and so on. But here I have no family.'

'What about your sister?'

'Leila?' He frowned. 'Leila is angry with me. Very angry. I do not want to ask her. And I don't think she would be very willing to help me, not in this.'

'Well, I'm not sure that I –'

'It is advice that I need, Señora, only advice. And I thought that you, as a woman, would know about these things. How it is done here.'

105

'Well . . .' She paused. 'I am not sure that I do. I am from Morocco.'

'But that is precisely why you would understand. You have taken the step yourself.'

'Step?'

'Of marrying a foreigner.'

Chantale felt uncomfortable. 'Well, actually . . .' And then enlightenment dawned. 'Ah! So you are intending to marry someone – not from Algeria?'

'That is it! Precisely it. She is Spanish. She is the daughter of a business acquaintance of mine. I have seen her when visiting his house. And I have decided to make her my wife.'

'I – I am not sure it is as straightforward as that, Abou – it is Abou, isn't it?'

He nodded. 'Abou, yes.'

'It is not quite the same as it would be in Algeria. Or Morocco.'

'Ah, good! That is what I wanted to know.'

'Have you any idea as to how she feels about it?'

'How she feels about it?'

'Yes. That is important here, you know.'

'Well, I haven't had a chance to ask her – I did not wish to speak to her until I had spoken to her father first.'

'Well, you see, he will want to know how she feels.'

'Surely she will be guided by him?'

'Well . . .'

'He knows me. He knows that I am a man of honour. And can provide for her.'

'Ye-es, but it is not quite the same thing. You see, Abou, one thing I have learned is that here in Spain much depends on how the woman feels.'

'She will surely be pleased –'

'Inclination comes into it much more than it does with us. A woman may see that a man is a man of honour and can provide for her but still not wish to marry him.'

'But that would be foolish of her!'

'It probably would. But that's the way it tends to be here. A woman follows her heart. It is not just honour and position. Her heart has to go with it.'

'Well, that is quite right. Her heart *should* go with it. But will that not follow afterwards?'

'It may do. But here a woman has to be inclined *first*.'

Abou thought for a moment.

'It worries me,' he said. 'I think people here are too ready to follow their inclination. There is no restraint. It has shocked me sometimes. I have thought it, well, promiscuous. The way some women behave! And men, too. It cannot make for a good marriage. A woman should enter marriage spotless –'

'There is much to be said for your point of view,' said Chantale cautiously.

'But the one I have in mind *is* spotless. She is pure and innocent and truly modest. She casts down her eyes before men –'

'Abou, how old is she?'

'Old? I do not know. Thirteen, fourteen.'

'In Spain that would seem too young to get married.'

'I *could* wait, I suppose.'

'That might be a good idea.'

'For a year. If we were contracted.'

'That would give you an opportunity to get to know her and for her to get to know you.'

'But I go back to Algeria in a week!'

'These things take time,' said Chantale neutrally.

Abou seemed cast down.

'I had hoped . . .' he said. Then he squared his shoulders. 'Perhaps I will speak to her father all the same,' he said.

'You do that.' And then, with a gush of pity:

'Abou, do not be disappointed if he says no. It will not be your honour that he doubts. It is just that the way they do things here is different.'

'So I see.' He gave a despairing shrug. 'Sometimes here,' he said, 'I feel lost. You do things that are obviously

107

right. And then they turn out not to be right! Leila is angry with me. But how could I know? I did what would be right at home, but things are different here. Leila herself has changed since she's been here. She is not the Leila I knew!'

Following their visit to the prison, Manuel had been making inquiries of his own. The tip that it was possible to get private supplies of food into the cells gave him something to work on. In the end it would have had to come in through the warders. Kitchen staff brought food to the floor in covered containers and left it there for the floor warder to deliver to the cell. The warder it had to be and Manuel had soon been able to identify the one. And here Manuel had had a great stroke of luck. One of the girls who worked for him, little Rosa, had a sister-in-law who was a remote cousin of the warder Enrico's wife. Among the Catalonians such relationships, however remote, counted for a lot and Manuel had used the sympathetic Rosa – made even more sympathetic by the belief that the inquiries were being made on behalf of the bereaved father so that it was in the cause, said Manuel, of a trust that was almost sacred – to put out feelers.

She had learned that something was definitely not right with Enrico and hadn't been right for some time, since, in fact, the formal investigation had begun. He had not been eating properly and had been drinking, correspondingly, far too much. His mother was very concerned about him and had urged him to go to Father Roberto and make confession.

Enrico had responded roughly and said that if everyone made confession who should make confession then Father Roberto would have a busy time. The mother had enlisted the aid of Enrico's wife, who was equally uneasy about his permanent, or so it seemed, loss of appetite, not just for food but for other things as well. His wife had put it down to some malign pressure in his bowels, a giant tumour perhaps, and had indicated to Rosa with considerable vivid pantomime, but probably rather less accuracy, the likely whereabouts of the tumour. She had even summoned the doctor. Enrico had, however, spurned the doctor as he had the priest, saying that doctors were only interested in extracting money from poor men and that he would be damned if he would let the doctor have anything to do with him.

Both his mother and his wife had crossed themselves at this and his mother had renewed her insistence that he go to see Father Roberto. Enrico had stumped out and taken to drinking even more heavily, and mother and wife were now at their wits' end. The time was therefore ripe, thought Manuel, for a discreet approach.

He had made the approach, very cleverly, through one of Enrico's drinking cronies, a long-standing friend whom the warder trusted; and he had used the card yet again of the father grieving for his son. It was not a case, said Manuel, of a family seeking to take revenge – so Enrico need not worry – but of a father needing to set his mind at rest. Information was all he sought, and for that he might be prepared to pay. Of course, said Manuel sternly, one should not accept money for such a sacred service as this, but . . .

Enrico said sod the sacred service. The money, on the other hand . . .

But could it be kept secret? He didn't mind doing the old chap a favour – it was only right that he should do what he could to make it easier for the old boy – but he didn't want to find himself caught and landed before the investigating prosecutor.

No chance of that, said Manuel confidentially. The information could be conveyed only to an ignorant Englishman who knew nothing about the set-up and so wouldn't ask awkward questions. He was interested only in putting the old man's mind at rest.

And wouldn't it set Enrico's own mind at rest? Anyone could see that his mind was troubled, had been troubled for a long time. In fact, too many people could see that and were, perhaps, beginning to ask questions. Put the old man's mind at rest, and then, perhaps, that would put Enrico's own mind at rest. He would have done what he could. And there would be no need for either priest or doctor and it would get his mother and his wife off his back.

This was a powerful argument and gradually Enrico became convinced. He had, after all, as he said to Manuel, nothing – much – to hide. He had been an innocent party to someone else's trickiness. He certainly wouldn't have passed the stuff into the cell if he had known – he had thought it was just sauce, something that would improve the God-damned awful food that the poor bastards were served with, make it a bit more tasty. No one had been as surprised as he had been when . . . It was all that damned woman's fault.

Damned woman?

Yes, the damned woman who had given it him and tricked him into passing it into the cell.

Enrico had been willing eventually, and after much per-suasion by Manuel, to talk to Seymour. The question, though, was where. Not in the bar, certainly, in front of his cronies; that would be asking for trouble. Somewhere pri-vate, secret? Seymour's room in the hotel? Enrico was reluctant: in fact, he was reluctant about any suggestion which would take him away from his own pitch and on to foreign ground.

But why did it have to be foreign ground, asked the ever-resourceful Manuel? Could not the meeting take place in Enrico's own home?

In front of his wife and his mother? Enrico shuddered at the thought. But then, gradually, came round to the

110

thought. He himself wouldn't have to do anything (always a welcome idea, that). The meeting would be completely private – he could tell them to get out of the house while the meeting was going on, couldn't he? Of course, he could, said Enrico confidently.

Chapter Eight

And over-boldly: for, when Seymour entered the room with Manuel, he found mother and wife sitting there, very much in occupation.

Manuel looked at Enrico, Enrico looked back at Manuel and shrugged. And so the meeting went ahead.

'This is an English Señor,' said Manuel. 'He has come not on his own behalf but on behalf of a grieving father who has lost his son.'

'Poor man!' said Enrico's mother, much moved.

'Poor man!' echoed his wife. 'Just think, Enrico, if we had lost our Simon!'

'Where is the little bugger?' said Enrico. 'You've made sure that he is staying out of the house?'

'He is playing with Ramon.'

'That's all right, then.'

Enrico turned to Seymour.

'So, Señor,' he said, a little uncertain of himself in this strange situation and therefore belligerent. 'What can I do for you? I cannot take long. I'm a busy man.'

'This will not take long. I want to know how the poison got into the cell.'

'Poison!' said Enrico's mother, crossing herself. 'You did not tell us that, Enrico!'

'How was I to know it was poison?' protested Enrico. 'I thought it was just a dainty. Something to give the prison food a bit of flavour.'

'You've always said that the food there is terrible,' supported his mother.

'Well, it is. And he'd been in for a few days and wasn't eating anything. The last two meals I had taken him he had just left.'

'That goes to show!' said Enrico's wife. 'If a man is hungry and still can't eat it, that tells you what the food must have been like.'

'I thought I was doing him a good turn,' said the warder.

'And so you were!' said his mother warmly. 'So you were.' She frowned, however.

'If it's that bad, Enrico,' she said anxiously, 'perhaps I ought to put something in a pot? Then you could take it in and give some to everybody.'

'No, I couldn't!' snarled Enrico. 'This is a prison, not a bloody hotel.'

'Our Lord bids us to take care of all those in need,' said Enrico's mother piously.

'Look, I'm just a warder, not the bloody caterer!'

'There's no need to swear at me!' said his mother severely.

'Even the beasts of the field,' said his wife, timid but supportive, 'need their food.'

'Animals now, is it?'

'So, Enrico,' said Seymour, intervening swiftly, 'when you were given the food to take in, you did not know it was poisoned?'

'Of course not! Do you think I would –'

'My son would never do a thing like that!' said the warder's mother, shocked.

'No, no. I didn't mean –'

'Enrico's a good man,' said his wife indignantly.

'What was it?' said Seymour. 'A pie, or something?'

'Yes, with a good crust on it.'

'That the way I do them,' said his mother approvingly.

'Enrico likes a good crust,' said the wife.

'Look, can you keep out of it?'

'I'm just wondering, you see,' said Seymour quickly, 'how it was done. For the poison to work, he'd have to have taken quite a lot of it. So the dish must have been tasty –'

'Oh, it was!'

His wife looked at Enrico suspiciously. 'How do you know that, Enrico?'

'Well, I tried a bit, didn't I?'

'Oh, Enrico, you might have been poisoned!'

'So I might! The bastards! They should have known I might have a taste.'

'But, Enrico, it was not your pie!'

'He was always putting his fingers in,' said his mother fondly, 'even when he was a child.'

'I didn't put my fingers in! I just took a bit of the crust.'

'It was a mercy you didn't.'

'And there was nothing unusual about the taste?' asked Seymour.

'A bit sour, perhaps.'

'He always likes it sweet,' said his wife.

'Or about the smell?'

'Not that I noticed. Mind you, you wouldn't notice, not with the general stink in there.'

'Do you collect the plates afterwards? How was he then? Did you notice?'

'He was sleeping. At least, that's what I thought. I don't collect the dishes straight away, I go in a bit later. And there he was, huddled up in a corner.'

'Poor man!' said his mother, sympathetically.

'He wasn't in there for nothing, you know,' said Enrico. 'So let's not bother too much about him.'

'How was the food actually given to you?' asked Seymour.

'She gave it me that morning as I was on my way to the prison.'

'She?'

'Yes.'

114

'A woman?'

'That's usual when it's a she. She had talked to me the day before. As I was on my way home. She stops me and says, "You're Enrico, aren't you?" "That's right," I say. "And you work in the prison?" "I do," I say. "On the third floor?" she says. "You've being doing your home-work," I say.

'She smiles. "Maybe I have," she says. Then she holds a hundred peseta note up in front of me. "I've got a brother in there and I don't think he's eating enough. So I wanted to get something to him. Something that would tempt him, you know. If I gave it you, could you see that he gets it?" "Well, I could," I say. She smiles again, and waves the note. "A hundred now," she says "and two hundred afterwards."

'"For your brother?"

'"That's right," she says. "Cell number five."

'And then I knew she was lying. Because I knew who was in the cell, and it was an Englishman. And she was speaking Spanish, so he couldn't be her brother,' said Enrico triumphantly.

He shrugged. 'But what the hell did I care? Spanish or English, as long as the note was all right.'

'I expect she was in love with him,' said his wife.

'Perhaps she was his wife,' said Enrico's mother.

'Not his wife,' said Enrico.

His mother clicked her tongue reprovingly.

'I expect she loved him passionately,' said his wife, brooding.

'Well, that's as may be –'

'I expect there was a file in that pie. So that he could file through the bars.'

'Look, there aren't any bars. There isn't even a window.'

'She would do anything for him. She would lay down her life –'

'Yes, well, she didn't, did she? She laid down his.'

This checked her. But only for a moment.

115

'She loved him,' she said, softly. 'She loved him passionately. And then he betrayed her.'

'Look –'

'And so she killed him. As I would kill you, Enrico, if you betrayed me.'

'You don't need to worry about that –'

'What about Conchita?'

'Conchita?'

'She's always standing at the corner waiting for you.'

'No, she's not. She's just on her way to the baker's to get a loaf for the evening meal.'

'She makes eyes at you.'

'The shameless hussy!' said his mother indignantly.

'I should be so lucky!' said Enrico: mistakenly.

'Ah! So it's not just on her side? You've had eyes for her, too?'

'No, no –'

'I shall kill her!' cried his wife.

'Quite right!' said his mother.

'Hold on a minute –'

'You don't love me!' cried his wife. 'You have betrayed me. I will kill her!'

'Now, look –'

'Let's leave Conchita out of it,' said Seymour, mistakenly, too. 'Let's go back to this other woman –'

'*Another* woman!' cried Enrico's wife. 'You are not a man but a beast!'

'Look –' began Enrico despondently.

As they walked away from the house Manuel was silent. He seemed to be thinking something over. He had not expected this, he said then, not this bit about the woman. She had obviously been employed, he said, for the occasion. A woman would attract less attention and it would seem more natural, he said, for a woman to be wanting to pass food in than it would have been for a man. A minor accomplice, he said: any woman would have done.

But he backed off quickly when Seymour asked him if it was possible for him to make further inquiries and see if he could find any clue to the woman's identity. Seymour did not press him. Manuel had done more than could reasonably be expected already. But, given his initial enthusiasm – he had, after all, volunteered his services – and given what he had already done, Seymour was surprised. And then an idea came to him: could Manuel be backing off because he had suddenly thought where such inquiries might lead?

'Señor Seymour!' cried the governor of the prison, with what appeared to be genuine pleasure and – or had Seymour got it wrong? – a definite relief. The relief on second thoughts, and perhaps much of the pleasure, could have been to do with the fact that the governor's desk was covered with sheet after sheet of numbers.

'I hope I am not interrupting you?'

'You are,' said the governor. 'Thank God!'

Seymour recognized the situation. 'Budget time?'

'You've hit on it. And now what can I do for you? There must be –' with a hint of desperation – 'something I can do for you to take my mind off –' he looked around him – 'all this?'

'Well, as a matter of fact –'

The governor almost rubbed his hands.

'Oh, good!' he said. He broke off to go to the door and called for coffee.

'How are you getting on with your inquiries?'

'Oh, progressing. Progressing. And how is the report of the investigation into Lockhart's death getting on?'

'Oh, progressing,' said the governor.

They both laughed.

117

'I shall not ask you about it,' said Seymour, 'but there is a little point – you will certainly think it a little point – which I would like your help on.'

'Big things I probably can't help you on; little things, just possibly I may.'

'You will probably think this trivial, and, anyway, there may not be a record of it: but while Lockhart was in the prison, did he have any visitors?'

'Señor Seymour, I am mortified to have to tell you – yes, he did.'

'Why mortified, Señor?'

'Because it reveals all too clearly the situation in the prison which my superiors falsely believe I have under my control. I think I told you that as soon as I found out that Señor Lockhart was among those admitted, that he was, in fact, in my cells, I sent someone down to see him. So I did. And it was then – then only – that I learned that he was dead. Well, I couldn't believe it. I summoned the doctor – I think I told you I summoned the doctor?'

'You did.'

'And it was only then that the full enormity of what had happened was revealed to me. But this was several days *after* he had been admitted, and all that time I did not know that I had Señor Lockhart in my prison. *I* did not know, but – but it appears that half of Barcelona did! That is what is so mortifying! There were no fewer than three requests to be allowed to visit him. I have only just found that out. Following your visit the other day I went back through the papers. And it was then that I found the records of the requests.'

'The requests were not granted, I presume?'

'Two of them were granted. The third was from a lady known to me. Known, in fact, to all of Barcelona. Known as one of the biggest liars in Catalonia! I turned it down. Goodness knows what might have got out if she had had a word with him!'

'This lady – her name wouldn't be Dolores, by any chance?'

'My God!' said the governor. 'You don't mean – you don't mean that you already know about her? Have, perhaps, talked to her?'

He struck himself a blow on the head with the heel of his hand. 'But that means she has been telling everybody about what she saw in the prison! Even though she didn't see it!'

'Actually, Governor, I think it's possible that somehow or other she may have wriggled her way in.'

'Oh, my God!'

The governor took a great gulp of the coffee that had now come in.

'It fits,' he said, sunk in gloom. 'Didn't I tell you, when you came before, that I was surrounded by anarchists? There are anarchists everywhere. In prison, out of prison. Spain, I sometimes think, consists entirely of anarchists. And they are all bent on subverting the system.'

'Tell me about the other two,' said Seymour, 'the ones you did allow in.'

'Not I,' said the governor. 'I had nothing to do with it. My subordinates – my alleged subordinates – agreed it without reference to me.'

He hesitated.

'I think I can understand it,' he said. 'One of them was an important lady, the wife of a very important person, high up in the Administration, and I don't think they felt that they had much choice: if they wanted to stay in their jobs. At least, that is the impression she gave them.'

'You couldn't give me an idea of her identity, I suppose?'

'No,' said the governor decisively, 'I couldn't. Because if I did, my own wife would never let me hear the last of it. The lady knows her and would be round to our house in a flash. No.' He shook his head regretfully, but firmly. 'No, I couldn't. Life would not be worth living. You see, Señor

Seymour, there is a kind of romantic solidarity among Spanish women.'

'Especially where Señor Lockhart was concerned.'

'Exactly. Especially where Señor Lockhart was concerned.'

'And the other lady? She was a lady, I take it.'

'She was, but this was rather a different case. It was made on compassionate grounds. By Señor Lockhart's daughter.'

'Señor Lockhart's *daughter*?'

'Or so she claimed. And I think there may have been some truth in it. For although every woman in Barcelona who wasn't Lockhart's mistress claims to be his daughter, I think in this case it may be with more justice. Or so I gather from the police at Gibraltar and, more reliably, my wife.'

'Her name?'

'I do not think that would help you, Señor. For while it is a good, honest Spanish name, it is not the name of her true father. A matter of considerable joy to the ladies of Barcelona. Including my wife.'

'It is true,' admitted Hattersley, 'that he did – well, put himself about a bit. There *were* rumours about the child. A daughter, I think. And yes, I've heard the other story – about the wife of the high-up official. Not to mention,' he said with a wink, 'plenty of others. And some of them were true. I can vouch for it myself. But I'm not so sure about those two. Still, if you've had it from the governor . . .'

They had met Hattersley on Las Ramblas.

'Yes,' he said, 'I am switching a lot between the two just at the moment – between Gibraltar and Barcelona. I'm having a big argument with Spanish Customs, and British, too, but the Spanish are worse. They take up more time. But I'll get there, I'll get there.'

He had suggested a coffee and taken them to a little place they had not discovered, where you sat outside and

120

had a good view right along Las Ramblas. And it was there that Seymour had put it to him.

'These two women,' he had said, 'have you any idea who they might be? The daughter, I think I might know; but the other?'

'I couldn't put a name to her,' said Hattersley, 'but I've heard the story. The wife of a high-up. On the judicial side, I think. But, you know, there are always these stories and, in fact, I have my doubts about this one.'

'Why?' asked Seymour.

Hattersley hesitated.

'Well,' he said, 'on the whole, in recent years at least, he's not been that taken by Spanish women. By women, yes, but not Spanish women. Some people say it goes back to the one he had the child by. A difficult customer, apparently. Prickly, certainly. The trouble was, she was devout.'

'I can see that might cause difficulties,' said Seymour.

'Well, yes. And why he got entangled with her in the first place! And she was married, too. Already, I mean. Well, of course, it didn't make things easy for her and she certainly didn't make things easy for him. Since I've known him, he's tended to steer clear of Spanish women. I used to tease him about it. If you are going to have these affairs, I would say, why don't you pick a beautiful Spanish woman? A Catalonian, for example, since you're so fond of them. There are lots of lovely women in Catalonia.

'"But they are all so virtuous!" he would say. "And religious!"

'I think that came from his previous experience. "It just makes for a lot of trouble," he said. Well, I don't know much about it really. I'm a bit of a bachelor, confirmed, myself. But I'd noticed, you see, that although he was unfaithful to Leila, he always seemed to go for someone like her. That striking Arab look. A bit like you, yourself, if I may say so, Miss de Lissac. Lockhart would have fallen for you in the first five minutes.'

'Well, thanks!' said Chantale, laughing.

121

'You may not think it, Miss de Lissac, but Leila Lockhart was quite like you when she was young. Shorter, yes, and smaller all round. But the face, the eyes, the dark hair, and something in the manner. Anyway,' said Hattersley, becoming embarrassed, 'he always *used* to fall for people like you. And Leila. He was faithful, you could say, in his own fashion.

'I spoke to him about that, too. "Why do you always choose Arab women?" I asked him once. "Do I?" he said, surprised. "Yes, you do," I said. He thought. And then he said, "Well –" and I do not know whether he was serious or whether he was joking – "perhaps because it is piquantly transgressive." "What?" I said. I was still a young man then and very innocent and I genuinely did not know what he meant. Of course, he knew that and I think he may well have been teasing me.

'"Transgressive," he said. "Crossing borders. Conventional ones, usually. Which pretend to be moral and are not. I think it is because I am an Englishman."

'Well, I knew then that he must be joking.

'"No, no," he said, "I'm not. My parents were very traditional and very strict and very English, even though my father came from Scotland. He was a soldier and had almost always been stationed abroad. In India, mostly. And there it was very bad form to take a native woman seriously. Sleep with them, yes, that was permissible. But marry one! No, no, quite out of the question. You would have been – what is the expression? Drummed out of the regiment.

'"But it wasn't out of the question for me," Lockhart said. "In fact, it was very much in question. I was about fifteen at the time and all women seemed beautiful to me. Especially the Indian ones. I wanted them so badly, and once I almost fell in love with one. It was very serious. At least, it was for me. Perhaps not for her. But certainly for my father. He packed me off back to England and sent me to what he called a good school, which would bring me up to be like him. I've always had a thing about schools since. I've even started to put my money into one – one which would *not* bring children up to be like him. That's Lockhart's blow for humanity!

'"You see, I didn't want to be like him. I wanted to be different. I cut away as soon as I could and I went to Africa, to Arab Africa. Anything to get away from the stifling conventions my father wanted to confine me in. And there, of course, I fell in love again. With Leila. And decided to marry her.

'"My father nearly went mad. Which, of course, made me even more determined. He threatened to cut me off. I said, thank God for that, and stayed where I was and married her.

'"So there you are. That's the answer to your question. Why did I go for an Arab? To show, at least to show myself, that I had broken loose from my father and all he stood for. And just that act of doing something major that he didn't approve of, that he had positively forbidden, gave me a great surge of freedom. Well, a surge of something or other. I thought it was freedom but it was probably sexual.

'"So there you are: that is why I like my Leilas. And perhaps why, although I am at bottom faithful to her, I am always looking for new ones. Each time, it gives me that same thrill of energy. Of course, it doesn't last, it never does. And then I go back to Leila."

'"You know, old man," I said, "I find that a bit shocking."

'He laughed. "You know, I find it a bit shocking, too. Because if it is true, it means that my father has won after all. I can't break loose. For, or against, I just can't break free from his influence. The old bastard!"

'Well, as I say, he was probably teasing me. And maybe he didn't confine himself to Arab women as much as I have suggested. Come to think of it, that is certainly so. His favours were broadcast and not confined to women who looked like Leila. No, definitely not. So maybe I'm wrong to discount this story about the wife of the high-up. He would probably have enjoyed it. The higher up, the better.

'But all the same there is something in what I said. He *did* have a strong preference for Leilas. So much so that we made a joke of it. Whenever we saw him with another one we would say, "Ah, there's a new Leila!"

'And when we saw one without him, we would sometimes say, "Hello, where's Lockhart?"'

Hattersley looked at Chantale.

'So you see, Miss de Lissac, that could be what people who know Lockhart think when they see you. "Another Leila: where's Lockhart?" Seeing you, they see him. That may be why they look at you in the way that you say they do. Where's Lockhart? And perhaps they wonder, seeing you, if this is just another of his tricks. And if, perhaps, this is a signal that one day he will be coming back.'

When Manuel had so suddenly backed off from making further inquiries, Seymour had thought that it might be because he had become afraid of where those inquiries might lead. Seymour had wondered for a moment if Manuel had been afraid that they must lead to Dolores.

Could Dolores have been the woman who had talked to Enrico and persuaded him to take the food in to Lockhart? Seymour could certainly see her doing that. She had tried to get in to see him in the prison – she had, actually, succeeded in getting in to see him in the prison. She could be, he saw, despite her scattiness, a determined woman. When thwarted, she did not give up. And she might well have tried to get food in to him, in the same way as one takes fruit to someone in hospital. Yes, he could see her doing that, and working out who the relevant warder was, and finding out a way of intercepting him and working on him.

But he could not see her wanting to poison him. Nothing that she had said to Seymour had made him think that she was anything other than genuinely in love with him.

124

Could it be that she had been in love with him but that something had happened to turn her against him? But, again, nothing that she had said had led him to think that. He went over in his mind all the conversations they had had and no, nothing in what she had said had even hinted at that. The reverse, if anything: poor, romantic Dolores seemed as stuck on Lockhart as she had ever been.

But could she have given the warder something unknowingly? Not knowing that it was poisoned? Well, yes, she could. If she thought it was something which would help Lockhart, she would certainly have been ready with her services and she would certainly have carried it through.

But equally certainly, probably even more certainly, if afterwards she had suspected what she had been used to do, he couldn't see her letting it rest. He was convinced that her passion for Lockhart was genuine and, if she thought that she had been tricked into killing him, it would surely have come out. This was something on which she could not, would not, have remained silent.

And, whatever else she might be, she did not seem to him stupid. She was intelligent enough to add two and two together. When she had known that Lockhart had been poisoned, she would, if she had had a role in it, have realized what she had done. No, she couldn't have done it knowingly and, if she had done it unknowingly, she would not have been content to let it rest there. Dolores, he thought, could be ruled out.

So if Manuel had backed off because he had been afraid of where his inquiries might lead, it was not on Dolores' account. On someone else's account, then? Manuel himself had said that the woman, whoever she was, had been merely a pawn, used by someone else. Who? Who else might Manuel have been shielding? Or, rather, the interests of what group of people might he have feared for?

Chapter Nine

When Seymour got back to the hotel, Chantale said, 'Your friend has been here again.'

'My friend?'

'The Chief of Police.'

'What did he want to see me about?'

'He didn't want to see you; he wanted to see Nina.'

'Again?'

'Can't seem to keep away from her.'

'Did he talk to her?'

'Briefly. Very briefly. I think she sent him away with a flea in his ear.'

Seymour looked out from the balcony. The school was winding up for the day.

He went down.

'You again!' said Nina.

'Me again,' agreed Seymour.

'I have nothing to say to you.'

'Ah, but you have. About your father, for instance.'

'My father?' said Nina.

'Lockhart was your father, of course.'

'How did you know?'

'You visited him in the prison. As his daughter. The governor told me. And I had guessed it from other things.'

'I begin to think,' said Nina, 'that it would be better to let my father rest in peace.'

'I think other people are coming to that conclusion.'

'Who?' said Nina derisively. 'The authorities?'

'Leila.'

'Leila?' said Nina, surprised.

'So I gather.'

Nina needed to think about this.

'If I were Leila,' she said, after a moment, 'I would never do that.'

'I wonder if she thinks the same about you.'

'Leila hates me,' said Nina. 'She would prefer me not to be here.'

'Well, I can understand that.'

'So can I, I suppose. She could not have a child, my mother could. My mother thinks we ought not to let her see us. It is too painful a reminder, she says. But I have to go there if I am to see my mother, and she doesn't want to move from Gibraltar because her life has always been there: her house, her friends, such relatives as we have. She tries to keep out of Leila's way.'

'It is difficult, I can see that.'

'My mother thought that Leila was afraid – afraid that my mother would one day take him back. Lockhart. Well, there is no chance of that now.'

'Would you have wanted her to take your father back?'

Nina needed to think again. She needed to think longer this time.

'I don't know,' she said. 'Half of me wanted him to be with us. But the other half of me said that he had never been with us, he had always lived apart. At the time that made me angry. I wanted a real father, like everyone else, not a father-at-a-distance. But it wouldn't have worked. He wasn't that kind of man. And perhaps my mother wasn't really that kind of woman, she just liked to imagine that she was. And perhaps I am not that kind of daughter. I think, actually, I am certainly not that kind of daughter. I was always glad to see him, but we never got on for long.

We would argue, quarrel. He thought I was too bitter. He thought I had been in Barcelona too long.'

'Yes,' said Seymour, 'that was what I wanted to know more about.'

'Me in Barcelona?' said Nina incredulously.

'You in Catalonia.'

'Isn't that the same thing?'

'I think you could live in Barcelona for a long time and not be aware that you were also living in Catalonia.'

'You would have to be blind!'

'Aren't many people blind?'

'Why are you asking me about this?' she demanded.

'Because the first time I heard of you was when Hattersley told me about you and the coffins.'

'Ah, the coffins!' she said, laughing. 'We wanted to make an impact.'

'Well, you certainly made one. Not just on Hattersley but on the British Foreign Office. Not to mention the British Navy. And even the British police.'

'Did we?' said Nina, surprised. 'In Barcelona we didn't even make the newspapers. But then, we wouldn't, would we?'

'You were afraid that people would forget Tragic Week. The authorities were afraid that they would remember.'

'Well, I'm glad,' said Nina. 'I'm glad that the ripples went so far.'

'The thing is,' said Seymour, 'the people you were doing it with were Catalans.'

'Well?'

'Not anarchists.'

'We were doing it for everybody that fell during Tragic Week. And plenty of those were anarchists, I can tell you!'

'But the people you were doing it with were Catalans.'

'It happened so, but –'

Seymour shook his head. 'I don't think it was an accident that the people you were doing it with were Catalans. They were the ones who, in a way, it was all about. It was

128

the conscription of Catalans for service in North Africa that sparked it off, that led, ultimately, to all the terrible things of Tragic Week. It was not such a central concern for the anarchists. They just jumped on the bandwagon. As did the Arabs in the docks, although they had the excuse that any crackdown by the authorities would almost certainly be aimed as well partly at them. No, in the end it was the Catalans who were behind it. And it was the Catalans that you were working with to see that it was remembered.'

Nina shrugged.

'So?' she said.

'Why was your father out on the streets during Tragic Week?'

'To see that the Army didn't get away with murder.'

'The Arabs think he was out there to see that the Army did not pick on them.'

'He was out there to see that they did not pick on *anybody*.'

Seymour shook his head.

'I don't think so,' he said. 'I think that your father was out there for a particular purpose. And it was a Catalan purpose.'

'Well?' said Nina. 'He was sympathetic to the Catalans. He admired the Catalans. He *believed* in the Catalans. As I do.'

'Up to what point?'

'I don't understand you.'

'How far was he prepared to go? What was he prepared to do for them?'

Nina did not respond.

'He was prepared to go pretty far,' said Seymour. 'He was prepared to go out on to the streets for them in Tragic Week. But was he prepared to go further?'

'I don't know what you mean,' said Nina.

'Was he prepared to supply them with arms, for instance?'

Nina turned her back and started to walk away.

'Was that what the Chief of Police was asking you?' said Seymour.

Seymour found the Chief of Police, as he had expected, sitting in the bar on Las Ramblas.

'The reason why I spoke to her,' said the Chief, 'is that I worry about her. As I would about my own daughter. "She's like a daughter to me," I said to Constanza. That was probably a mistake. You see, God has not blessed us with children and Constanza is sensitive on that point. "Oh," she said, "like a daughter, is she? Are you sure she's not like someone else? A wife, for instance? Or a mistress?"

'"Constanza," I said, "how can you say a thing like that? You know I am faithful!" "I know you're stupid," she said, "and just the sort of man to fall for a chit of a girl when she makes eyes at you."

'"You are unjust to her," I said. "No one in their right senses would say she'd make eyes at me. Rather the reverse."

'"Oh?" she said. "So you've been disappointed, have you?"

'"No," I said. "I'm just pointing out what anyone can tell you: that the only thing between us has been harsh words. Whenever I try to help her, all I get is rudeness."

'"Playing hard to get, is she?"

'"Not at all," I said. "She's a child alone, without a father, and has a mother far away, in Gibraltar or some place, and as difficult, from what I hear, as she is."

'"And you want to step in," she says, sneering, "and be a father to her, is that it?"

'"She needs a father," I say.

'"Oh, yes!" she says. "Well, you're a bigger fool even than I thought. You think she's taken a fancy for your big moustaches, I suppose!"

'"Leave my moustaches out of it!" I say. Although they *are* rather fine.

'"How can I leave them out," she says, "when you go waving them at every pretty girl you see!"

'"I have *not* been waving them at Nina. As I told you, it's just that I feel for her as I would for a daughter."

'And then she flies off the handle and stamps out!'

'Well, there you are, Chief!' said Seymour. 'That's a woman for you.'

'That's my wife for you,' said the Chief gloomily.

'So when I heard you warning Nina that day, you were doing it just out of the kindness of your heart?'

'That's right. As I would do for a daughter. Although I would hope that any daughter of mine would not be like Nina.'

Seymour laughed. 'I think I can understand that, Chief! But, tell me, you must have had grounds for your warning?'

'Oh, yes!'

'You said that she was mixed up with a bad lot?'

'Oh, yes. A very bad lot!'

'Anarchists?'

'The lot of them!'

'I ask, you see, because I understand from the prison governor that he has a lot of anarchists in there. And that they were there when Lockhart was there.'

'Ah, yes. They would have been arrested at the same time. In Tragic Week.'

'Was that awkward for you?'

'Awkward?'

'Well, I rather gathered from what you said that you'd had your eye on them in connection with something else. And if you were already deep into an investigation, having to shovel them into prison like that may have cut across your inquiries.'

'Well, it did – I thought that we were getting somewhere. Of course, you can say that if they're in prison then they landed up in the right place, even if it's for something else.'

131

'Yes, but – correct me if I'm wrong – but I thought your original investigation was into something very, very particular.'

'Well, it was.'

'What sounded to me – from what you said to Nina – a possible murder.'

'It could turn out to be that. It could very well.'

'A man died.'

'He did, he did.'

'Ramon Mas.'

'Ramon Mas.'

'And you thought that Nina's friends might have been mixed up in it.'

'Not "might"; they definitely were, the bastards!'

'Could you tell me about it?'

'They were all in it together.'

'Smuggling?'

'Of course! Everyone's into smuggling on this coast. That is, all the fishermen. There's not much money in fishing, you see. To keep a family alive, you've got to have good money coming in. So they all do it. A boat goes out in the middle of the night and meets another boat, and something is handed over. There's nothing to it. And they really think there's nothing to it, it's completely natural to them. They've been doing it for years, for always. They don't even see that it is wrong. Against the law? The law? What's that? Never heard of it. Don't believe in it. They're anarchists, as I said. All of them.'

'Not Catalan Nationalists?'

'There are no Catalan Nationalists in Spain,' said the Chief automatically.

Chantale joined him and they continued along Las Ramblas. They ran into a group of *cabezudos* and stood for a while watching them lollop around. They were playing with some children, giving them rides on their shoulders

132

and taking part in their skipping games, pretending to be clumsy, stumbling and even falling. The children shrieked with laughter.

Despite their bonhomie there was something slightly frightening about them, he thought. Partly it was their size. Seymour was tall himself but they towered over him. To the children they must have seemed giants. And yet it didn't appear to bother them. They were used to them, he supposed. But also, perhaps, he thought, they fitted naturally into a child's world, among the giants and the ogres and the fairies good and bad. They had something of the ambivalence of figures in folk stories, creatures who were unpredictable, as adults were sometimes unpredictable, as their parents occasionally were.

The *cabezudos* were a bit like that for adults, too. They might turn out to be good or bad, could give a helping hand or could lead you astray. They were not to be relied on. They had been pretty helpful to him, but was that just something to gain his confidence so that he could be tricked later? That was what the woman had suggested when they had first encountered them.

They seemed to know everything that was going on: about him, for instance, and what he was doing there; about Lockhart and what he had been up to; about – for that, surely, was what the tip about Lockhart's interest in fish was meant to convey – the smuggling. They seemed to have tap-roots into everything, especially if it was in any way underground.

Who were they?

Locals, certainly, and therefore, and from their speech, Catalans. Nationalists? Or was that the wrong sort of question to ask? Did they reach back past modern political organization into deep folk tradition?

Or were they not so much Nationalists as anarchists? There was a sort of disruptive spirit about them, an opposition to authority and all that was order. To the authorities, certainly. But they didn't seem to be anarchists in the way that he was used to, anarchism as a political form – the way that Nina was, for example. It was more spontaneous than that.

Whose side were they on? They had seemed to be on Lockhart's side. Why? Was it because they recognized in him a kindred free spirit? Or was there some closer, more practical tie? A commercial one, perhaps? Or a sympathy they and Lockhart had in common? Or both?

As one of the cabezudos skipped past him, he murmured, 'I'm looking for Ricardo.'

The *cabezudo* gave no sign of having heard and danced away. A little later, though, it returned and said, 'You don't look for Ricardo. He looks for you.'

'All right, tell him to look for me, then.'

The *cabezudo* capered off and soon the whole group of *cabezudos* had moved on. Seymour knew that they would find him if they needed to and he and Chantale walked on.

They found a little restaurant tucked away down by the harbour, almost on the quay. It didn't look much of a place, consisting of a few, bare, untableclothed tables, but it was crowded and they had difficulty in finding a table. It was a busy place. Waiters in black trousers were dashing about armed with bottles and baskets and some of them were bringing out black earthenware pots from the kitchen, which they placed on the tables. As they lifted the lids off delicious smells spread though the restaurant. The pots all contained fish of some kind: sardines, mullet, bass, but also mussels and lobsters and shrimps.

'You have chosen the right place,' said a voice beside them.'

It was Ricardo. He dropped into a chair beside them. 'You permit?'

'Please join us,' said Seymour.

A waiter put a pot on the table and three plates. The pot

contained a mixture of things, squid, shellfish and great lumps of fish: a sort of fishmonger stew.

'This is where the fishermen eat,' said Ricardo. 'Also the people who work in the fish market. And many others, too.'

'Provided they are Catalan?' suggested Seymour.

Ricardo gave him a quick look.

'Provided they are Catalan,' he agreed.

'It is just that I have been listening to the conversation,' said Seymour.

'Ah, yes,' said Ricardo, 'you have a good ear. And now, perhaps, that you have been here for a while, you are beginning to tell the difference between Catalan and Spanish.'

'The fishermen are all Catalan?'

'Mostly.'

Seymour picked a shrimp out of the pot.

'Was Ramon Mas a Catalan?' he asked.

'Andalusian, I think.'

'But definitely not Catalan?'

'Definitely not,' said Ricardo. He signalled to the waiter and he put a bottle on the table. It was the local wine, strong, rough, and with a bit of a tang.

'Why are you interested in Ramon?' he asked.

'I was wondering if Lockhart was interested in Ramon,' said Seymour.

'Not very,' said Ricardo.

'Someone told me he gave money to Ramon's family.'

'Did he?' said Ricardo. 'Or was it the police?' He shrugged. 'Perhaps it was Lockhart. He was always a generous man.'

'Tender heart?' suggested Seymour.

'Why, yes,' said Ricardo. 'A tender heart.'

'Too soft,' said Seymour, 'to bear grudges?'

The waiter had brought a basket of coarse, thick, brown bread. Ricardo took one of the pieces and dipped it into the juice at the bottom of the pot.

'It was not so much that,' he said. 'These people can't afford to bear grudges. They are very poor. So poor that they have no choice other than to be realistic. If they see their livelihood threatened, they have to take action.'

'Ye-es,' said Seymour, 'I see that. But Ramon was poor, too.'

'Desperately,' agreed Ricardo. 'But he thought he saw a short-cut, you see.'

'Was it that?' said Seymour. 'Or was it that he did not entirely share everyone else's belief in what they were doing?'

'That is possible,' conceded Ricardo.

'He being an Andalusian,' said Seymour, 'not a Catalan?'

'It is possible.'

'What,' said Seymour, 'was it that they were smuggling?'

'Smuggling?' said Ricardo.

'A traditional pursuit along the coast,' said Seymour, 'and not one which, I would have thought, Ramon would ordinarily have objected to.'

He waited.

'Probably not,' said Ricardo.

'Nor Lockhart either,' said Seymour. 'But, then, I can't see why Lockhart would have been interested in smuggling, anyway. A bit small beer for him. Unless, for him, it wasn't entirely to do with profit.'

'For them, too,' said Ricardo. 'They may be poor, but it wasn't just money. They are proud people. They have beliefs and ideals and values, too.'

'Arms?' said Seymour. 'For the Catalans?'

Ricardo hesitated.

'Was he selling them to you?'

'No,' said Ricardo. 'It wasn't like that. We went to him because we knew he could arrange it. With all his contacts.'

'Along the coast,' said Seymour. 'And in the military?'

'Not so much the military,' said Ricardo, 'as with their suppliers.'

'Of course. And with his sympathy for the Catalans.'

'We paid for the arms,' said Ricardo, 'we didn't pay him. He did it because . . .' He shrugged. 'Well, because he felt the way these poor, brave men do.'

Chantale tied a scarf around her hair and went down alone, without Seymour, to the little market beyond the soot-blackened church. It was an Arab market, of course, and she felt quite at home. She studied the fat tomatoes and squeezed the luminous aubergines and gazed long at the melons. There, too, she talked to the veiled shoppers in their long, dark burkas and compared notes. And she talked to the stall-holders and asked them about the provenance of their products. Were they local or had they come from 'the other side', from Algeria or Morocco?

Or Tangier, even? She herself came from Tangier. But she and her husband were thinking about moving over to 'this side'. Was there scope here for a small fruit business? She had heard that it was hard but that in the long run you could do well. 'That might be so,' said the stall-holder she was talking to, but he had been here for six years and found that the run was longer than he had hoped.

'It is like,' he said, 'a bird on a cliff. It can find a niche to build its nest and lay its eggs. But there is not much room on the ledge and the fledglings still have to go somewhere else to fly.'

'There is not much money here,' said the woman beside her, 'even for the Spaniards.'

'More than there is in Morocco, though,' said another woman close by.

Chantale nodded.

'So they say,' she said.

'But I haven't found it yet,' said the stall-keeper. 'The Spaniards buy from their own.'

'And keep to themselves,' said the woman beside Chantale.

'You find that?' said Chantale. 'We were told that it would not be like that.'

'Depends what you're selling,' said the stall-holder, 'and where you are.'

'We were told there was a businessman here who might be able to help us,' said Chantale. 'An Englishman, not a Spaniard. His name is Lockhart.'

'His name *was* Lockhart,' corrected the stall-holder. 'He's dead now.'

'Dead?' said Chantale, as if shocked.

'He might have helped you. He helped a lot of people.'

'Arabs?' said Chantale.

'Arabs, too.'

'Even Arabs,' said the women beside them bitterly.

'That may have been his undoing,' said the stall-holder. 'They say he went too far.'

'In helping the Arabs?'

'People here didn't like it. And, you see, he wasn't a Spaniard himself. He was an Englishman. And they said, "What is he doing here? Always with the Arabs. But making money from the Spanish."'

'He was married to a woman from Algiers. She came from a big family there. They traded all along the coast. People say they were the ones who gave Lockhart his start.'

'Certainly he was close to them,' said the stall-holder.

'Until they fell out,' said the woman.

'Fell out?' said Chantale.

'When they heard he was playing around. With other women.'

'They sent someone over. A brother, I think.'

'But then it all got sorted out.'

'They say his wife forgave him,' said the stall-holder. 'It's best like that.'

'I don't know,' objected the woman. 'It's always the woman who forgives.'

* * *

Chantale was thinking about this as she walked back to the hotel. And then her mind moved on to the difficulty of carving out a new life in a new country. She was thinking about herself, of course, and about Seymour. She was always thinking of that these days. But today she was thinking less about herself and more about Seymour. Suppose, instead of her moving to England, he moved to Morocco? That would get rid of the difficulties, wouldn't it? At least from her point of view. She would have no hesitation about marrying him then. And he would manage all right in another country. She had seen him. He was at ease in Spain, as he had been at ease in Tangier. His own family had moved to England. His roots were not that deep in England.

But then, what would he do? She had asked herself that question before. He would have to find a job. What as? A policeman again? Not a chance. Neither the Moroccans nor the French, who now called the tune in Morocco, would have it. He would have to do something else. Set up a business, perhaps, as these people she had just been talking to had done. But what sort of business? She smiled. A fruit shop, perhaps? She couldn't see it. Either for him or for her.

The Arab men were still lounging at the corner. They looked at her as she went past. They looked at her with hot eyes and sullen faces. They made her feel uncomfortable and she hurried on past them and back up past the scorched church and out into the open, leafy space of Las Ramblas. There she felt better.

She met Seymour and they went back to the hotel together. Two women were talking in the foyer. One of them was the proprietress of the hotel, whose grim visage had daunted Seymour's hopes of the double room. She was always dressed in black. When she went out to the church, which she was always doing, two or three times a day, she covered her head and shoulders with a black shawl. He had never seen her smile.

But now she was talking animatedly to the other woman, as if they were old friends who had not met for a while.

And, indeed, he learned later, they were old friends. They had been children at a convent school together. Which was why, when Nina had moved to Barcelona, and began teaching at her school, her mother had written to her old friend and asked her to keep an eye on her. For the other lady, the one the proprietress was talking to, was Nina's mother.

She recognized him at once.

'Señor Seymour –'

'Señora!'

'The Señor is looking into Lockhart's death,' Nina's mother told her friend.

The proprietress clicked her tongue sympathetically.

'Ah, Lockhart!' she said, and shook her head.

'Even in death he will not leave us alone,' said Nina's mother.

The proprietress put her hand over Nina's mother's hand.

'Do not speak ill of the dead, Maria,' she said. 'With all his faults, he had a big heart.'

'But a small head,' said Nina's mother.

'And he loved his child.'

'Sometimes love is a curse,' said Nina's mother.

Later in the evening Seymour and Chantale came down the stairs. The two women were still talking, the proprietress now sitting at the reception desk, Nina's mother perched on a stool nearby.

'Would you like some calico?' she was saying. 'I've just had a chance to get some cheap . . .'

Chapter Ten

As they passed Manuel's café, on their way back after dinner that evening, Dolores came rushing out.

'Where have you been?' she said. 'He's sent me out twice to look for you!'

'Manuel?'

'And sent you a message! I know, I delivered it. I told him you weren't there, at the hotel, and he said, "Where the hell is he?" And he sent me out again, and I've been looking all over the place!'

Manuel appeared in the doorway. 'Ah, there you are! Look, this has been costing me. Four cups of coffee so far. Each! And Enrico keeps wanting me to add something stronger too.'

'Enrico?'

He remembered now: the warder.

'Not just Enrico,' said Manuel. 'They've all come.'

'All?'

'All the family. Wife, mother, even the children. Three! And little buggers, all of them. But I didn't give them coffee. I sent them out. "Either they go or I go!" I said. "All right," says Enrico, quick. "I'll take them down to the playground." "No, you won't!" said his mother. "There could be money in this!" "No, you won't!" said his wife. "There's a woman in that playground and you'll fall on her just as you did on the other one."'

'What *is* this?' said Seymour.

Manuel led him inside. There, at the table in the kitchen, were Enrico and his family, a row of empty cups before them.

'I got a message,' said Manuel.

'I sent it,' said the mother.

'I certainly didn't!' said Enrico.

'You were not to be trusted,' said his wife, bursting into tears. 'I shall never trust you again! Never! Never!'

'That a son of mine –' said his mother.

'Not a son, but a beast!' said his wife, through sobs. 'A ravenous beast!'

'Now, look here –' started Enrico.

'And a dirty Arab, too!' said his wife. 'That is what hurts!'

'That a son of mine –'

'Conchita first,' said the warder's wife, 'and then an Arab! How many more? Oh, how many more?'

'Disgusting,' said his mother. 'That a son of mine –'

'Look, I haven't done *anything* –' said the warder desperately.

'Not for want of trying!' said his wife darkly.

'*She* approached *me*!'

'And you surrendered at once!'

'No, I didn't! I just agreed to take him some food, that's all.'

'Ah, but was it all?'

'She gave me three hundred pesetas.'

'And what else did she give you, Enrico?'

'Nothing!'

'Three hundred pesetas is a lot of money,' said the mother, watching.

'She didn't give you herself, by any chance?' said his wife implacably.

'No, she didn't!' protested Enrico. Then, goaded beyond endurance: 'If only she had!'

'But we know this!' said Seymour. 'There's nothing new here. You all knew it.'

'Ah, but what we didn't know was that she was an Arab.'

'I thought she was a decent Spanish lady,' said Enrico's wife.

'Men are all the same!' said his mother.

'An Arab! You didn't tell us she was an Arab. You let me think that she was a decent, honest Spanish woman. Suffering because the man she loved was in jail! Prepared to do anything to help the man she loved! Smuggle in files to cut through the bars of his cell window –'

'There *aren't* any bars! There *wasn't* a file!'

'She would have been ready to die for him if necessary!'

'Ah!' said the mother, sighing. 'Women are like that.'

'And now you tell me she was an Arab!'

'That a son of mine –'

'No, no, don't start that again!'

'– should betray the trust placed on him by His Excellency!' finished the mother, eyeing her son balefully.

'And his country!' said his wife spiritedly.

'Look, you were all in favour of it!' said the warder. 'You wanted to send in pies for all of them –'

'Not for Arabs,' said his mother.

'To think of you talking to her!' said his wife. 'Fondling her –'

'*Fondling* her?' said her husband desperately.

'Very probably,' said his wife, facing up to things bravely.

'I never touched –'

'Beast!'

'All men are like that,' said his mother philosophically. 'Even my son!'

'Even your son!' echoed Enrico's wife.

'Not to mention his father.'

'My God!' said Enrico. 'You'll be bringing in Grandfather next.'

'Him too –'

'For God's sake!'

'Was that what you wanted to tell me?' said Seymour.

'We thought you would like to know. That she was an Arab.'

'Well,' said Seymour thoughtfully. 'You're right. I would.'

'Well, that's a relief!' said Manuel.

'You thought it was Dolores, didn't you?' said Seymour.

'What?' said Dolores.

'You thought it was Dolores who had given Enrico the poisoned food.'

'Yes,' said Manuel, 'yes, I did.'

'You thought –' said Dolores, stupefied.

'I am sorry,' said Manuel.

'You surely did not think . . . But that was a terrible thing to think!'

'I thought so, too,' said Seymour. 'For a moment.'

'That is awful! How could you even suppose –'

'I am sorry, Dolores,' said Manuel. 'Very sorry!'

'But I loved him!' she said.

'It was partly because I knew that you loved him,' said Seymour. 'Loved him so much. And thought that perhaps he did not love you.'

'Our love was not like that,' she said. 'We were not jealous of each other. We allowed ourselves things. I knew about him, he knew about me. And it didn't matter. We found that when we came together, it would be as it always had been. The others were just – flings. For both of us. Really he loved me.'

'Dolores –'

'Yes, he did!' she insisted. '"I'm just your bit on the side," I said to him once. "Yes, but you're my *special* bit on the side," he said. "you're like a second wife." There! You see? He said it. "In fact," he said, "if I were a Muslim and you were a Muslim and Leila would agree, I'd *make* you my second wife." So you see, I was his wife. Almost.'

'Dolores, Dolores!' said Manuel, shaking his head.

144

'I knew about his other women. Of course I did! But I didn't mind. They wouldn't last, I knew that. They never did. They never worried me. Except once. It was just before he died. He'd told me about this one. She was the wife of a high-up. She'd fallen for him, bang! Couldn't live without him. She said. But she would have to. She was already married. And she was a Catholic, too. These married women!' Dolores said, sighing. 'Always getting in the way!

'That what I told myself. She couldn't be a real rival. She couldn't be his wife. That's what I told myself. But then I thought – this was after my visit to the prison, after Tragic Week, when I was doing a lot of thinking – I thought that maybe she felt like me, maybe she felt as much as me. And I – I almost felt sorry for her.

'But then I thought, maybe she felt like me, and was just as jealous as I was. Because I was jealous, despite what I said just now. Deep down I was jealous. Very. And I thought maybe she was, too. And that maybe – maybe she had killed him. Because of that.

'And then I thought, maybe it wasn't her. It was him. Her husband. The high-up. Well, it could have been. He wouldn't have liked it, would he? And he could have done it, couldn't he? While he had Sam there, at his mercy . . . Well, he could, couldn't he? He could have done it.

'But then I thought, perhaps I was imagining things. I tried to put it out of my mind. But I couldn't. I kept imagining . . . and then you came,' she said to Seymour, 'and I thought, maybe he will find out. And I thought, if it is a woman I will kill her. And if it's a man, well, perhaps the authorities will kill him. And if they don't, I will.

'But then I thought, if it is this high-up, maybe he's got it all sorted out. I mean, why haven't they found him out already? It must be because they're not looking. Because this man, the high-up, has got it all fixed. And I thought maybe this new man, this Englishman, coming to it from outside, will get somewhere. Because they won't find it so easy to fix him.

'That is what I thought. But now the warder says the woman who gave him the food to take in was an Arab. So I couldn't be right, could I, about her? But I could still be right about him. The high-up. He could have got someone else to do it. It would be easy for him to get an Arab.

'I don't know what to think. I don't know what to think now.'

She burst into tears and Manuel led her away gently.

Seymour stepped down into the underground café. It was more full than it had been before. They were all Arabs, of course. He was conscious of them scrutinizing him surreptitiously. He hoped that they would recognize him and know that he had been before and that he had talked to Ibrahim, so that he had, as it were, credentials. The waiter came to him more quickly than he had done before and served him coffee, so that, perhaps, he thought, they did.

He didn't mention Ibrahim this time, just sat there.

A man went out and a little later Ibrahim came in and sat down beside him.

'You are still here, then?' he said.

'For just a little longer. Then I shall go back to England.'

'Did you speak to Leila?'

Seymour nodded.

'I think she plans to build a life here,' he said.

'Don't we all?'

'Despite losing her husband.'

'That is brave,' Ibrahim said. 'But perhaps she is right. Once you have made the step you shouldn't go back.'

Seymour looked round the café with its solely Arab clientele.

'Isn't this a kind of going back?' he said.

'Yes. But you can only go so far at a time. Later, perhaps, you will take another step. What was it you wanted to know?'

146

'I want to know if any of you visited Lockhart when he was in prison.'

Ibrahim made a little motion with his hand and the waiter brought more coffee.

'Why do you want to know?'

'Others did. I wondered if his friends did, too.'

'It was just after Tragic Week,' said Ibrahim, 'and most of us were lying low.'

'You must have talked together, though. And possibly about him.'

'We talked, certainly. And, when we heard, about him. There was a lot to talk about and many of us were in two minds.'

'About Lockhart?'

'Yes. But mostly about what was to be done. And we were still deliberating when we heard that he was dead. You have to remember this was just after Tragic Week and the police were looking for us. They were looking for others as well, of course, but it was thought best if they did not see us together for a while. So, for a while, the community was fragmented.'

'And then you heard that Lockhart was dead?'

'Yes.'

'And what did you think?'

Ibrahim shrugged. 'That a good man was gone.' He hesitated. 'At least, many of us thought that.'

'And some didn't?'

'Some didn't.'

'What did they think?'

'That perhaps it was best if it ended.'

'Even like this?'

'Even like this.'

'Did you think that?'

'I did not see how it could end like this.'

'Because . . .?'

'Because in the Arab world things like this never end.' He sighed. 'I sometimes think that is the reason why I am in Spain and not in Algeria. If you never let things end, what hope is there? And yet this is all so bound up with the way we are.'

'And the way Lockhart was?'

Unexpectedly, Ibrahim laughed.

'You could say that,' he said wryly. 'But in a different way.'

He touched Seymour's hand.

'But I'll tell you this,' he said. 'That is what Leila thinks. Let it end, she thinks. Let it end here. And I think that is why she will never go back. She wants to put it behind her, all that has happened, and not – not pursue it.'

Seymour nodded. 'I had a specific reason for asking if any of you had visited Lockhart when he was in prison. Perhaps I should have made it clearer: if any of you had visited the prison while he was there, not necessarily Lockhart himself.'

Ibrahim looked puzzled.

'I don't understand,' he said.

Seymour hesitated. How far could he go? How much could he rely on Ibrahim being on his, on Lockhart's side? He hesitated, and then plumped.

'Lockhart was poisoned in his cell,' he said. 'Probably by some food that the warder was given to take in to him. A pie, probably. The warder was given the food by a woman. She gave him money, too, to take it to Lockhart. The woman was an Arab.'

'An Arab?' said Ibrahim. 'Are you sure?'

'Yes.'

Ibrahim sat there for some time thinking. 'I am shocked,' he said. 'I do not know a woman from our community who could have done that,' he said. 'But, as I told you, after Tragic Week, the community was very fragmented. Even so . . .'

He thought some more.

'I do not know who it could be,' he said. 'Even though

there were disagreements among us over Lockhart, I find it hard to believe that . . .'

'Do you really find it so hard to believe,' said Seymour, 'knowing the kind of man that Lockhart was?'

'I know the kind of man that Lockhart was,' said Ibrahim, 'especially, and I think this is what you are saying, the kind of man that Lockhart was as regards women. But Arab women! It is not with Arab women as it is with Spanish women. Or English women, as far as I know. An Arab woman is hedged around. It is not easy for her to meet a man, let alone . . . Which is, I think, what you have at the back of your mind. Harder here, even, in some ways, than it is back in Algeria. We are a small community. Everyone knows everything. And we are, as I think you were suggesting earlier, defensive. We look inwards still. Too much. Not outwards. That kind of thing – our women – we are jealous of. It touches us closely. Our pride, perhaps, but also our fear. I find it hard to believe . . .'

'Nevertheless,' said Seymour, 'it was an Arab woman.'

Ibrahim sat there for some time turning it over in his mind. Then he said, 'Go away for a while. An hour perhaps. And then come back.'

Chantale, meanwhile, had been doing what she had taken to doing more and more when Seymour was away. She had gone out into the plaza and sat on a bench beneath a palm tree. At first when she had been left alone she had gone for a walk along Las Ramblas. The feeling of release and freedom which she had experienced on the first day was still with her; but she was beginning now to have a sense of horizons closing in, that things couldn't go on like this.

And, of course, they couldn't. Sooner or later, and sooner rather than later, Seymour would have to go back to London. And she?

Well, that was the old question, and it was still the question as she sat on the bench. Should she go to London with

149

him? Or should she go back to the place to which her inner strings still pulled her, to Tangier and her mother, and all the little things – the buzz of the bazaars, the fresh smell of mint tea from the cafés, the smells of the horses and donkeys and the strange, musky perfumes of the women, and of the men, too, often – which she was suddenly beginning to miss?

The truth was she was no further on in answering the question than she had been when she arrived. Should she marry Seymour? Well, yes, increasingly she thought she should. She was beginning to recognize – and this, perhaps, was progress – that she couldn't manage without him. But did that mean that she had to abandon all that was her life and go with him to some cold, dirty place she had no feeling for? Why couldn't he come to her? But she knew very well why he couldn't come to her. She had gone through that. And the idea of the halfway house for both of them, which had been at the back of her mind when she had agreed to come to Spain to see him – that wouldn't work, either. She thought of the expatriate Englishmen they had come across in Gibraltar. Did she want Seymour to become like them? No, she certainly did not!

And what about the Arabs she had met here? They, too, had made that leap from one country to another, looking for a better life. But had they found it? Few of them seemed completely at ease. They clung, or at least the Arabs she had met in Barcelona did, to vestiges of their old life. They remained, she thought, divided souls. But wouldn't she, if she went to England, be a divided soul, too? And so the debate she was having with herself went on.

Sometimes Nina would spot her on the bench and when the school had closed for the morning she would come across and sit beside her and eat the roll she had for lunch. They would talk. About what happened to Nina during the morning, about the children – but also about Tangier and Morocco and Algeria. Those places to which Nina's father had devoted so much of his life. Nina seemed hungry to know about that, as if by recapturing something of that she could recapture something of him.

Or, perhaps, understand him better. That was what Nina seemed to need, thought Chantale. She felt that Nina was puzzled by her father and could not understand why he had abandoned her. Especially as he seemed to love her. She clung to that. She was sure he had loved her; why, then, hadn't he wanted to live with her, as other fathers did, with their children?

Nina was very young, thought Chantale, suddenly feeling very old. What was puzzling Nina was people; what was puzzling her was love.

And Nina was coming to Chantale for enlightenment! To Chantale, who was probably even more perplexed, just at the moment, than she was.

This morning, while they were sitting on the bench, Nina's mother came across to them.

'Señorita?' said her mother, raising her eyebrows.

'Señorita still,' said Chantale firmly. 'Señora Seymour shortly. Perhaps.'

'It is better so,' said Nina's mother.

'Mother!' said Nina crossly.

'It is better so!' insisted her mother.

'It is probably better so,' conceded Chantale. 'But there are other things to be thought of too.'

Nina's mother leaned across and patted her hand.

'Of course there are!' she said. 'There always are.'

'It is not always possible to marry,' said Nina sternly, 'even if you are truly in love. As you found.'

'Ah, "truly",' said her mother. 'But how do you know?'

'Of course you knew!' said Nina. 'Surely you knew, Mother?'

'Oh. Yes. Both times,' she said drily.

151

'You wouldn't have wished it otherwise, would you?' asked Nina anxiously.

'I was a young girl the first time,' said her mother, 'and I didn't know either myself or him. The second time I was confident about both of us. Wrongly.'

'You weren't wrong,' said Nina sturdily. 'You loved him, and, despite it all, it was worth it.'

'Maybe,' said her mother, 'but I wouldn't wish it like that for my daughter.'

'What do you think, Señorita de Lissac?' appealed Nina.

Oh, God! thought Chantale. What *do* I think?

'Yes, what do you think, Señorita?' asked Nina's mother.

'I don't know,'said Chantale slowly. 'I don't know what I think. In all circumstances? But suppose the two are very different? The man and the woman? Perhaps even coming from different countries?'

'Yes,' said Nina's mother curiously. 'What then?'

'I think, in the end, I would follow my heart.'

'Quite right!' said Nina.

'Quite wrong!' said her mother. 'But –' she smiled to herself – 'it's probably the mistake I would make again.'

'Mother!' said Nina, laughing, and throwing her arms around her.

'Come with me,' said Ibrahim.

He led Seymour into a back room, where an old Arab woman was sitting on the floor.

'This is Um Hanafi,' he said.

'Greetings, Mother,' said Seymour courteously, in Arabic.

She wore the usual dark gown and headdress and was heavily veiled. Over the top of the veil he could see her eyes. She was blind.

'Um Hanafi knows everything,' said Ibrahim. 'Both here and in Algeria.'

'Morocco, too?' asked Seymour.

'Only the coast,' said the old woman.

'But Tangier?'

'Tangier, yes,' she nodded.

'Then you will know the woman I hope to marry. Her name is Chantale, and her mother is from the Fingari family.'

'I know her mother,' said the old woman. 'Her mother is a good woman,' she said to Ibrahim. 'And a strong one.'

'Her daughter is a strong woman, too,' said Seymour.

Um Hanafi cackled with laughter.

'Then you will have to be a strong man,' she said.

Seymour laughed too.

Then he said, 'You know what I want to know. And why I want to know it.'

'I knew Sam Lockhart,' the old woman said. 'I knew him in Algeria. But that was when I could still see.'

'And this woman,' said Seymour, 'the one who brought the poisoned food to the prison, did she know Lockhart, too?'

The old woman hesitated.

'I did not think she did,' she said.

'But you know her?'

'I think I know her. People have said – there were rumours even at the time. She speaks Spanish, yes?'

'Yes.'

'She has been here a long time. Ten years by my count. It has made her bold. Bold enough to do what you say she did. But still I am surprised. I did not know she knew Lockhart. Her father did, yes. But not her.'

She laughed again. 'Her father knew Lockhart too well to trust him anywhere near his womenfolk.'

'How was it that he knew Lockhart?' asked Seymour.

'They did business together. In the old days it was oil. But that was in Algeria. Then he moved to Spain. He settled in Tarragona,' she said to Ibrahim. 'That is why you do not know him.'

'But you think she did not know Lockhart? That puzzles me,' said Seymour.

153

'Yes,' she said drily, 'it puzzles me, too. But I think it was because Farraj – Farraj is her father – always kept himself separate. And he kept his family separate, too. "The world is changing," he said, "and we need to change too. Only not too much."' She laughed again. 'That was Farraj all over. Keep to the old; but try the new also.'

'Why do you think that she may be the one who went to the prison?' asked Seymour.

'She was seen. She was seen in Barcelona. Someone recognized her – they knew the family. They said, "Why is she here?" And they thought, If she is here, she will surely come to see us. But she did not, and they were surprised. So they asked after her. And then another person said they had seen her, too. Near the prison, right by the gate. As if she was going there. And they said, "Surely Farraj could not be there? Because if he is, we must go and see him." So they asked her, and she said, no, it was not Farraj. It was Lockhart, and she was taking something to him. And they came back and told others, and they said, "Perhaps we should do something." But then they heard that Lockhart had died. So they put the thought from them. But nevertheless, some of them remembered that they had seen Aisha, and wondered.'

'I would like to speak to Aisha,' said Seymour.

'That will be a hard task. For she is no longer in Spain. Her father sent her back to Algiers.'

'When did he do that?'

'Afterwards.'

'How long afterwards? Immediately afterwards? Or long afterwards?'

'Immediately after,' said Um Hanafi.

Chapter Eleven

Seymour noticed that some of the street names had been freshly painted out and other names substituted in their places. Often the change seemed insignificant: *avinguda* for *avenida*, *passéig* for *paseo*, *carrer* for *calle* – all basic names for thoroughfares, avenue, passage, street. But the changes were significant, all right. They were from Castilian, the usual, official, language of Spain, to Catalan. It was an attempt to assert Catalonia against Spain, another Tragic Week, as it were, only this time without bloodshed. The Catalonians had been defeated but they had not gone away.

Some of the names had been painted over again and the original, Spanish, name restored. But that wouldn't work. The language of the ordinary man here was Catalan. The fishermen spoke Catalan not Spanish, the language in the cafés was Catalan. Even the *cabezudos* spoke Catalan.

It was the Catalans throughout who had helped him. It was their effort at remembrance with the coffins in the church that had brought Lockhart to England's attention. Ricardo, throughout, had been on his side. And so, in their curious, elliptical way, had been the *cabezudos*. It was they, for instance, who had put him on to the smuggling. It was as if the whole underground side of Barcelona had been anxious that he should not miss the point about Lockhart. Lockhart, they were saying, was a Catalonian at heart. There are no Catalonian Nationalists in Spain, the authorities kept telling him. Well, that was plainly wrong, for Lockhart was one.

And that was why he had been killed, that was what they were all saying. They were anxious that he should get the message.

And, of course, the corresponding message was that it was someone who was opposed to the Catalonians who had killed him. Like the Spanish Government or its agents.

But Seymour was not so sure about that. That was clearly the message he was intended to get; but was it the right one? For one thing, if Lockhart had been a Catalonian Nationalist, he had been other things as well: an anarchist, or certainly an anarchist sympathizer. Seymour had no reason to think that his sympathies were not genuine. It was just that they didn't seem to be exclusive. He had had sympathy for *all* the underground causes.

As they were walking along they met the Chief of Police, also taking the air. He had a lady on his arm.

He detached his arm and bowed low. 'Señor, Señorita! Allow me to introduce –'

'Don't make such a fuss about it, Alonzo,' interrupted the lady.

'– Constanza,' finished the Chief hurriedly. 'My wife.'

'A pleasure to meet you, Señora,' said Seymour.

'I like to meet everyone my husband is working with,' said the Señora. 'That way I can keep my eye on them. And him.' She caught proper sight of Chantale. 'And sometimes it is a good idea,' she said severely.

'Constanza –' murmured the Chief deprecatingly.

'Mademoiselle de Lissac,' said Seymour.

'French?'

'Moroccan,' said Chantale firmly.

'Ah! You are very pretty, Mademoiselle. I am not surprised my husband has said nothing about you.'

'Constanza –'

'But, Señora,' said Seymour, 'he has said a great deal about *you*.'

156

Constanza laughed.

'I try to loom large,' she admitted. She turned to Chantale. 'Are you going to be here for long, Mademoiselle?'

'Probably not,' said Chantale.

'That is just as well.' She turned her attention back to Seymour. 'Does that mean you have found out who killed Lockhart?' she demanded.

'Quite possibly,' said Seymour.

'Ah!' said Constanza. 'That is something my husband never did.'

The Chief shrugged.

'It was just one thing among many on my desk,' he said.

'Ah! Your desk!' said Constanza. 'Many things finish up on your desk. Finish up and then never move again!'

'You are too hard, Constanza –'

'Did you know Lockhart, Mademoiselle?' Constanza asked Chantale.

'Not personally,' admitted Chantale.

'Well, that is a relief!' said Constanza. 'He seemed to know most of the attractive young women around here. Personally.'

'Including you, Señora?' asked Seymour.

'Including me, certainly. In fact, I knew him better than most.'

'That is quite a claim, Señora,' said Seymour.

'It is,' said Constanza, 'and perhaps we should start there. Would you care to give me your arm, Señor Seymour, for a little walk along Las Ramblas? And you, Alonzo,' she said over her shoulder, 'can walk with Mademoiselle de Lissac. Just walk. I shall be watching you. And keep fifteen yards behind. Exactly. Now, Señor . . .'

She put her arm through Seymour's. 'You think, then, that you have discovered who killed Sam Lockhart?'

'I am beginning to have an idea of that, yes.'

'Cautious, cautious! Well, that's something that Sam certainly never was. But you are beginning to? You think? Well, that is good! It is time somebody found out. The

157

thought that it could go unavenged partly because of my husband's bungling is intolerable!'

'You keep a pretty firm hand on your husband, don't you, Señora?'

'*Someone* has to,' said Constanza. 'Otherwise nothing would get done around here.'

'He has told me about your guidance during Tragic Week.'

'It caught us out,' she admitted. 'I didn't see it coming. And then when it did I nearly let Alonzo become involved in it.'

'You wanted him to keep out of it, of course. So that you could have a free hand?'

'It was not so much that, I always see that I have a free hand. I just didn't want him mucking things up.'

'You knew that Lockhart was out there, of course.'

'Of course. And he was another one I would really have preferred to keep out of it. Naturally. I told him so. "Sam," I said, "for God's sake, watch what you are doing. With all those tiles flying about, one of them may hit you. And it will probably come from me!" "Don't worry!" he said. "I shall be all right. I assure you I shall be functioning perfectly when I come to see you this evening. While your husband is sitting in the bar watching the pretty girls go by."

'But, of course, he didn't come to see me. Those imbeciles picked him up, along with everyone else, and put him in prison. "Alonzo," I said, "your men need a good kick up the backside. Apply yourself usefully for a change."'

'You visited him in prison,' said Seymour.

She looked at him in surprise.

'Yes, I did,' she said. 'How did you know that?'

'And talked to him. What did you talk about?'

'"Sam," I said, "this is no place for you. We've got to get you out of here." "I think that would be a good idea," he said. "But how?" "I'm working on it," I said.'

'And you tried to get him out?'

'Of course, I did! And would have too, if they had not been so incompetent. I put the fear of God into Alonzo. "Alonzo," I said, "you have put Lockhart in prison, and you know what will happen now: that dreadful Admiral will send in his warships and apart from blowing you to little bits, it won't make you very popular with Madrid. Let him out, quick!" Well, he would have let him out . . .'

'But,' said Seymour.

'Yes.' She went quiet for a moment. 'That's right.'

'He was killed.'

'Killed, yes. I never thought they'd catch up with him.'

'They?'

She made a sweeping gesture. 'Just about everyone. So it seemed at times. The Government – but they should be discounted on the grounds that they don't really have the ability to organize the killing of anyone. Although they might do it by accident, of course.'

'Señora, are you an anarchist, by any chance?'

'The anarchists, too,' she continued. 'Although they, of course, were very keen on him.'

'Did you know about Nina?'

'Not at first. Absurdly, I was jealous of her. For a little while I wanted to kill her. As well as him, of course.'

'And did you?'

'Nina, no.'

'And Lockhart?'

She laughed. 'Is that one of the little details you haven't quite got straight yet?'

And then she sobered up.

'Poor Lockhart!' she said. 'He didn't deserve to die. He was the one bright spark around here. Of my life, I may say! He was different from other men. Impossible, of course. But that was why I – we – loved him. Don Quixote born again! The Don Quixote of modern times! Charging around wanting to do good. Like all the other do-gooders. *I* am not a do-gooder,' she said.

'I had rather spotted that.'

'But although he was ridiculous, like the original Don Quixote, I suppose, he made life interesting. And that was the point. When you were with him he lit everything up. And you were part of it. Just for a moment, because that was about all the time he could spare for you before he moved on to the next woman. But it was worth it. Life suddenly shifted to another plane. And it was like that for all of us. All of us! He had that gift. He made life richer, suddenly lifted it up out of the tedious and humdrum – and, God, can life in Barcelona be tedious and humdrum! He was ridiculous, of course. With all his causes. But somehow he made you believe in them. For a bit. Even the Catalan cause! For God's sake!'

'You are not a believer in the Catalan cause yourself, then, Señora?'

'I believed in it for a bit. I would have believed in anything if he had asked me to. Even fairies. But only for a bit. And by the end he himself was having second thoughts about them. There was a nasty incident. A man was killed. Lockhart was very angry. And after that he went quite off them.'

'When was this, Señora?'

'It was about the time of Tragic Week. Or just before. "If you feel like that," I said, "why do you go out on the streets?" "To be fair," he said. "To be fair." I ask you! What sort of a reason is that? Where would the world be if fairness came into it? For God's sake!

'Anyway, you're missing the point. The point was that he was romantic. With all those mad enthusiasms of his, that out-of-control idealism. He was a regular Don Quixote, always tilting at windmills. Well, me, I'm normally on the side of windmills. Good, solid things with plenty of money coming out of them.

'But every so often you get fed up with down-to-earth, solid things. Like my husband. You want to fly up in the air, get away from them. Give romance a chance. Even if you know it will probably end with you falling back to earth with a bump.

'When you were with Lockhart, you believed that romance had a chance. That perhaps you could escape. That things didn't have to go on the way they were. You really believed you could fly in the air. You abandoned the windmills and went for Don Quixote. Despite yourself. Despite everything. You felt you had been given a chance of life.

'Well,' she said, 'I went for Don Quixote. And now the bastard is dead. Damn him, damn him!'

'Señora,' said Seymour, 'you visited the prison once: did you visit it a second time?'

'No. I was waiting until I had got things set up for his release.'

'And you didn't send someone else instead?'

'No,' she said, surprised. 'Why would I do that?'

'You didn't try to send anything in to him? For his comfort? Food, for example?'

'Food? No.'

Then she suddenly realized. 'What are you saying? That I tried to poison him?'

'I wondered if you had used someone else. Another woman. An Arab woman.'

The Chief's wife drew herself up. 'Señor Seymour, if I had wished to poison Lockhart, I would have done it myself. I would certainly not have used a dirty Arab woman to do it!'

When they got back to the hotel they found a message from Hattersley. It asked if they would mind dropping in at his office. 'This afternoon if possible.' As an afterthought, Hattersley had scribbled on the bottom of the message: 'It really is rather urgent.'

He had said 'they' and so they both went. He seemed relieved to see them.

'Terribly sorry,' he apologized. 'Such short notice! But – but it is rather urgent. His note came only this morning, and he is going back to Algiers next week.'

'This is Abou, is it?' said Seymour. 'Leila's brother?'

'Yes. And he particularly asked – since he would be going back so soon – if I – we – that is, if you agree – could get on with it.'

'What is it?'

Hattersley looked at Chantale. 'I gather he has already spoken to you about it?'

'What exactly?'

'His plans for marrying.'

'Well, in a general way . . .' said Chantale.

'Oh? I gather from his note that he had been more particular.'

'He rather poured his heart out, yes.'

'Ah!'

Hattersley seemed relieved.

'He's rather poured his heart out to me, too,' he continued. 'I mean, I don't know anything about it really.' He went pink. 'Never done it myself, I mean. Asked anyone to marry me. Could never quite pluck up courage. And, I suppose, there's never been anyone –'

'Has he asked you,' said Chantale, 'to act for him?'

'Well, yes,' said Hattersley. 'In a way, he has. And I wouldn't want to – to let him down.'

'No, no. Of course not. But I really don't see where we come in –'

'He has great respect for you, Miss de Lissac. He says you have made the step. Already bridged the gap. Between Africa and Spain. He thinks they might listen to you.'

'Me?' said Chantale, aghast.

'I told him – in confidence of course – that you were very highly thought of in London. That, of course, was why they chose you to come out here. That, as far as he was concerned, confirmed it. If they accepted you, wouldn't he accept you?'

162

'He?'

'Señor Vasquez. The father of, well, what he hopes will be the bride. I know Vasquez, of course. We've been in a few things together. A good man, a good man for business. He knows me and I know him. We trust each other, you know. That's very important for business. And I suppose Abou knows about our relationship and that's why he asked me. Probably seemed like a good idea to him – I know Vasquez, and he knows me. Well, that's fair enough, and if it was a question of business, I'd be happy to oblige. But marriage! Phew!'

He blew out his cheeks. 'I think maybe he guessed that was how I would feel, because it was then that he went on to you, Miss de Lissac. Mentioned your name. Said he'd already talked to you about it and that you'd been very kind. Helpful, he said. And understanding. Well, I'm sure that's true, Miss de Lissac, but, in my experience, that's not the sort of thing Arabs would usually say about women. So I think he must have been really impressed by you. Understandably, of course. Understandably.

'So I don't think he would mind if – I'm sure he wouldn't, since he's spoken so warmly of you – and mentioned it in the first place – if I asked you to give me a bit of help.

'I wondered if we could go round together and see him? Señor Vasquez, I mean. And you, too, old chap. I mean, the more the merrier. Or, no, I don't mean that, I mean it would lend weight. And Abou would be pleased.

'And if you could do the talking. Once I'd introduced you, I mean. The fact is, I wouldn't really know what to say.'

'I don't think it is appropriate,' said Chantale. 'For us to be active in this. It is the family's responsibility.'

'Yes, but he hasn't got any family here. Apart from Leila, that is, and he says she is angry with him and wouldn't do it. And, in any case, is it a thing for women? You would know this better than I, Miss de Lissac. But Abou seems to feel that it is a man's job. Or would be in Africa. To conduct the negotiations, I mean.'

'Look, I don't think it is going to get to negotiations. He'll turn it down flat,' said Seymour.

'Yes, but . . .' Hattersley wriggled. 'All we can do is put it to him. And then find a way of letting Abou down as gently as possible. And you will do this so much better than I would. I feel that now he has asked me, I've got to do it. Have a shot, you know. Although I'm sure you're right, it's hopeless. Out of the question. But I've known the family for so long, the Lockharts, I mean, that I feel I need to do *something*. But without you, I'd be lost. I wouldn't know what to do. Miss de Lissac, would you, *could* you, please . . .? And you, too, old chap. Because I need some support. By God, I do!'

Seymour and Chantale took the train to Tarragona. Hattersley, and Abou, would have to wait. There were more important things to do. Like seeing Farraj.

From the outside there was little to distinguish the house from all the others in this prosperous district of Tarragona. It was only when you got inside that you realized that this was an Arab house. The floors were tiled and uncarpeted. The carpets were on the walls, thick Persian ones with intricate geometrical decoration, which took the place of pictures. There were, too, some beautiful Persian vases, standing in niches, but otherwise the rooms contained few objects apart from beautifully worked leather cushions which took the place of chairs.

Seymour and Chantale were led, however, through to a tiny inner courtyard in the middle of which was a fountain, and scattered around the courtyard were orange trees in tubs, filling the courtyard with their sweet scent.

Farraj was sitting beside the fountain reading a book. He rose to his feet when Seymour and Chantale were shown in and bowed courteously.

'Your name was mentioned,' said Seymour, 'as that of one who could help me.'

'The Book tells us that if help is solicited, it should not be refused,' said Farraj.

'It is not asked for lightly,' said Seymour.

He introduced Chantale as someone who was helping him. Farraj, who had deflected his eyes politely so as not to look at her directly, now registered her presence, again with the slight shock that she had noticed in the other Arab men she had met here. He recovered and bowed courteously.

'And how can I help you, Señor?'

'I am inquiring into the circumstances in which someone died. An Englishman. From Gibraltar. His name was Lockhart.'

'I knew Señor Lockhart.'

'Well, I believe?'

'Years ago, very well indeed. Of recent years less well. Since our move to Tarragona. We exchanged greetings regularly but seldom met.'

'What I have to ask now is difficult. For me and perhaps for you.'

Farraj looked at him inquiringly.

'It concerns your daughter.'

'Aisha,' said Farraj: neutrally but, Seymour fancied, guardedly.

'Who, I understand, is no longer with you?'

'She returned to Algiers. To get married.'

'And is she married now?'

'Happily, yes. To an old friend of mine.'

He looked at Chantale involuntarily. Chantale understood the look and didn't mind. It wasn't like the Chief of Police's looks. This assumed that she was married and noticed only that it was not to an Arab.

She knew that it was improper, as a woman, for her to enter into the conversation herself, but couldn't resist saying, 'And are there children?'

She had half expected disapproval, or even reproval. Strangely, however, he seemed to seize on her question with relief.

'We have indeed been blessed,' he said. 'She has two children already!'

'And both boys?' said Chantale, somewhat ironically, assuming, from the fact that they were blessed, that they must be boys.

'One boy, one girl. I know what you are thinking, Señora, and I assure you I would have been nearly as happy if they had both been girls.'

'This is, perhaps, the great blessing,' said Chantale.

'That is what Aisha would have said!'

Talking to Chantale, he seemed to relax.

'I had feared – she was getting rather old, you see, and showed no inclination to get married. "There is time enough," she said. But she was nearly thirty! And no one seemed to please her. It didn't seem to bother her. "It is different here," she said, and I think she relished her freedom.' He shrugged. 'But there came a time when it became expedient for her to go back to Algeria, and then I was able to arrange marriage for her. With some difficulty,' he added. 'Since she was so old and so . . . unbiddable, I was going to say, and that would not be right, because in the end she fell in with my wishes. Independent, shall I say, as young women here, in my experience, seem to be.' He looked at Chantale again. 'And you, yourself, Señora? Have you children of your own?'

'Not yet,' said Chantale, feeling a bit uncomfortable, as if she was committing herself too far.

'May you also be blessed!'

'Your daughter left for Algeria shortly after Tragic Week, I gather?' said Seymour.

'That is so, yes.'

'She was not involved in the events of Tragic Week herself?'

'No, no, no, no! Certainly not!'

'I wondered if her sympathies had been involved?'

'Sympathies?'

'I wondered what had driven her to try and smuggle a present to Lockhart in his cell.'

There was a long silence.

'You know that, do you?' said Farraj eventually.

'Yes.'

Farraj sighed. 'I was against it. But ... she was persuaded.'

'Who by?'

Farraj gave no sign of having heard the question.

'It was little that she was asked to do. And she remembered Lockhart from the old days. He used to sit her on his knee. As a child,' he added hurriedly. 'As a child! "I know you don't think it right, Farraj," he used to say to me, "but in Scotland it *is* right!" And I didn't mind. She was just a child. But she remembered those days, and she felt sorry for him. And, yes,' he sighed, 'I suppose she did feel for those involved in Tragic Week. It was hard not to feel caught up in it. Even I, even I ...! And you must understand that we had friends in Barcelona. In the docks. I did a lot of business there. And when we heard the dock people were among those being shot down ... So, yes, perhaps it was not too difficult to persuade her. Her sympathies *were*, as you say, involved.'

'But she also had feelings for Lockhart, you said.'

'Oh, yes.'

'And so she would not have known what she was passing in to him?'

'What *was* she passing in to him?'

'What killed him.'

'She certainly did not know that,' said Farraj quietly.

'And you, did you also not know that?'

Farraj looked at him levelly. 'No. I suspected. Afterwards. When I heard that he had been poisoned. And heard the rumours. But not before, Señor, not before. And if I had, I would not have let her do it.'

'Why, then, did you hastily send her to Algeria?'

'Because she told me the little she had done. And I saw at once that she would be implicated. I did not want her to suffer. Who knows, with the Spanish police, what she might have had to undergo? And even if she was released, what she would still have to suffer afterwards? What hope would there be now of marriage? Better to get her out, and, fortunately, I was able to find an old friend who didn't mind. Who was prepared for my sake to marry her.'

As they were leaving, Seymour said, 'And you are not going to tell me who persuaded her to do it?'

Farraj shook his head firmly.

'One does not betray one's own kind,' he said.

Back in the hotel, Seymour was sitting in the vestibule waiting for Chantale to come down so that they could go out to dinner. He heard footsteps on the stairs and looked up. It wasn't Chantale, however, but Nina. She hesitated for a moment and then came over and sat down beside him.

'My mother will be down in a moment,' she said, as if this boldness needed explanation.

'And so I hope, will Chantale,' said Seymour.

There was a slightly awkward pause. Nina did not seem to invite conversation but he thought that this was awkwardness, shyness, perhaps, rather than hostility.

'You have had a good day at school?'

'Every day is a good day at school.'

'You have found your vocation, clearly.'

'Yes.'

There was another awkward pause.

'It is a responsibility,' said Seymour, 'and a rather demanding one, I would think. Are there just the two of you?'

168

She fired up defensively.

'We can manage,' she said.

'I am sure you can. Certainly the teaching. I have seen you, and am most impressed.'

She looked at him suspiciously.

'No, I mean it. I certainly couldn't do it.'

'Men are less good at this sort of thing,' said Nina forgivingly.

'And what about the administrative side? Do you have to do that as well?'

'We have a parents' committee.'

'And that is all?'

'Anarchists do not believe in unnecessary administration. We are opposed to bureaucracy.'

'Yes, of course. I was just wondering if you had any support from outside.'

'We don't need support from outside.'

'I was thinking of the chance to share views, pool experience.'

'Well, that might be wise,' said Nina, considering. 'But there aren't any other anarchist schools near us.'

'There are anarchists, though?'

'Oh, yes. It is a growing movement.'

'And do you have much contact with that wider movement?'

'We are too busy, really. Perhaps we should.'

'You sound very much on your own.'

'Anarchists believe in self-reliance.'

'Yes, of course. But sometimes ploughing a path of your own can be very lonely.'

'Esther and I support each other. And we get support from the parents. Perhaps,' she admitted, 'not a lot of support. But Esther says that is always the case with parents.'

'And your father, how did he fit in? Was he part of the wider movement or was he just, well, interested in the school? Because you were?'

'Well, I think he was generally interested in anarchist education. He was interested in education of all kinds. Perhaps because he thought that, having been to an English public school, he had never had one. But, perhaps, yes, he was particularly interested in what we were doing because it was me.'

'He didn't put you in touch with anarchists outside?'

'No, no. He didn't really know many anarchists.'

'You know, that surprises me. What about the fishermen? Aren't they anarchists?'

'Well, they are and they aren't. They have a lot in common with anarchists, they are against authority, for example, and very self-reliant. But they are not – not very theoretical. Well, you wouldn't expect it. In fact, my father rather liked that. "They're practical people," he used to say. "They just get on with it." I don't think he talked much about anarchism with them. They're not – not the sort of people to have that kind of conversation.'

'Do you have that kind of conversation with them?'

'Not really. They're very conservative. They don't really talk much to women they don't know. They don't talk to anybody much, really.'

'So your father's contacts with them were not really anarchist contacts but more a matter of business?'

'Not just business. He liked them and tried to help them. He gave them money sometimes.'

'And then, of course, there was the smuggling.'

Nina stood up.

'Señor Seymour,' she said, 'I think you're fishing for information.'

Chapter Twelve

'Hmm,' said Señor Vasquez, 'I don't know about this. He's a nice man, I'm sure. I ran into him occasionally in Gibraltar. I've always got on well with him. But I don't know how Carmen might feel. Or her mother, come to that.'

'Well, that's it,' said Seymour.

'It's important how your daughter feels,' said Chantale.

'Well, it is. And she's got a mind of her own. I don't know, well, how she would take to it. I mean, it's a fear, isn't it? Their ways are not our ways – I don't mean anything by that, Señora,' he said hastily, turning to Chantale. 'If they loved each other, that would be enough for me. But there's always the worry, isn't there, how things might work out? Marriage is difficult enough anyway without – without complications.'

'I feel that, certainly,' said Chantale.

'Of course, if you knew him better . . .' said Seymour. 'The family, that is.'

'Well, yes.'

'Unfortunately, he's going back to Algeria in a week.'

'He is?' said Señor Vasquez, brightening.

'I think he was hoping to get some sort of agreement before he departed,' said Hattersley.

'Agreement?'

'Or acknowledgement.'

'Well . . .'

'I told him that things could not be rushed,' said Chantale.

171

'No, certainly not,' said Señor Vasquez. 'In Spain there is normally a long courtship. That gives the couple a chance to know each other. And, of course, it eases some of the natural doubts of the families.'

'A wise custom,' said Seymour. 'Provided it's not extended for too long.'

'Although there are risks in shortening it,' said Chantale.

Señor Vasquez looked at her gratefully. 'There are, Señora, there are! On both sides. For both families.' He hesitated. 'You are, if I am not mistaken, Señora, from appearance, not unconnected with the family yourself?'

'Distantly,' said Chantale. 'Distantly.'

'Distance sometimes gives perspective,' said Señor Vasquez.

'Of course, you yourself, Señor, I gather, from what you said, know him quite well?'

'Well, not *that* well. As well as one knows anyone one meets primarily through business. And business is – well, rather different, isn't it?'

'It is. But did you not have an opportunity, while you were over in Gibraltar, of meeting his family? Seeing him in something of a family setting?'

'I met his sister. Charming lady. Very businesslike. But –'

'And did he not sometimes come over here?'

'To Barcelona? Yes. Yes, occasionally. The docks. We sometimes used to meet over business in the docks. The Lockharts have an office there. And once I invited him round to our place for lunch.'

Once, thought Seymour? Was the whole edifice of Abou's hopes built on one casual visit only?

'It seemed kind to. He always struck me as being rather on his own.'

'He was probably feeling rather lost. Had he been to Barcelona before?'

'Once or twice. But then he was here for a week or so just before Señor Lockhart died. Business was building up, I suppose. He was here during Tragic Week. You know

172

about Tragic Week? It must have been quite a shock to him. But, of course, if you were doing business at the docks, that was just the time when you needed to be there. And then, of course, when poor Señor Lockhart died, he was here a lot. He had to step in for a considerable while.'

'And when Señor Lockhart was in prison – you know he was put in prison?'

'Along with a lot of other people.'

'Yes, along with a lot of others. Was Abou about then?'

'I never quite understood what happened during that week. Or what Lockhart was doing. They tell me he was out on the streets. In the middle of all that! It seems crazy to me. But I suppose he felt – felt that the bullet would not hit him. A dangerous assumption, that.'

'But, of course, it didn't. Or doesn't seem to have done. He was just arrested.'

'Well, I think he was lucky,' said Señor Vasquez. 'And, I am afraid, rather foolhardy.'

'Was Abou in Barcelona at that point?'

'I think he came over later in the week. The office probably sent for him. Well, there was business to attend to, down at the docks, and I don't think Lockhart was paying much attention to that. Or perhaps that was how their manager felt, so he sent for help and Abou came over. Just in time. Because then Lockhart was arrested.'

'Señor, Señor!'

It was the Chief of Police who was hailing him. He came up to Seymour and took him by the arm.

'Señor, I have to speak to you. To correct an impression you may have received. It is a false impression, Señor. You know what women are! They talk, they talk, and they embroider. It was not like what she said to you the other day. It is not, believe me, the way she pretended it was. It is a game with her, Señor. She likes to tease me. What she said, however, was not true.

173

'All the stuff about Señor Lockhart! It is true that she knew him. Well, she'd met him once or twice. But not the rest of it. About him and her. She says it sometimes, but that is just to provoke me. And so it was on this occasion. She was showing off to you, and trying to annoy me. I could hear what she was saying, and she was speaking loudly enough for me to hear. She *wanted* me to hear.

'She does that. Makes comparisons. To my disadvantage. Romantic, she used to call him. "He has the spirit of a true romantic," she said to me once. "He has the spirit of a true trouble-maker," I said. "Unlike you, Alonzo," she said. "You have no spirit of romance." "I have better things to do," I said. "Like sitting in a bar," she said.

'"Anyway, it's not true," I said. "I *have* a spirit of romance. I like the flamenco girls as much as anyone." "This is quite different," she said. "That is sex, not romance. At least, in your case. I never said you were without appetite, Alonzo. Performance may not always be up to scratch, especially after you've had a few drinks, but I have never said that you were without appetite. However, it is of the earth, earthy. Like the peasant that you are at heart, Alonzo. You do not lift your eyes from the furrows that you hope to plough, as in the case of the flamenco girls. Whereas Sam Lockhart –"

'"– had an appetite, too," I cut in.

'"No doubt about that," she said, laughing. "Well, you wouldn't want a man without one, would you? Or where would women be? But the point is, a woman looks for something more than appetite. A man who brings colour into her life. A man who has dreams. A man whose horizons extend beyond that of the nearest bar."

'"If all men limited their horizons to the nearest bar," I said, "there wouldn't be half the trouble that there is."

'"And there wouldn't be half the excitement that there is," she said. "And the world would be a much duller place."

'"My job is to keep it dull," I said.

174

'"And mine, I think," she said, "is to liven it up a little. You stand for order. But I am coming to think I have a little too much order in my life. I want to kick over the traces. I need a bit of disorder."

'"You have the spirit of a *cabezudo*," I said.

'She laughed. "You know," she said, "I think you could be right. The trouble is, you want to put all the *cabezudos* in jail."

'"Well, I do. The world would be a better place without them."

'"Well, thanks!" she said.

'"But not you, Constanza," I said quickly. "I make an exception for you."

'"You may be wrong in that," she said.'

In the little harbour the boats were busy. They would soon be putting out to sea for the night's fishing. The fishermen were checking their nets. Seymour walked round apparently casually but listening carefully.

They were all talking Catalan. It was as he had expected. Nevertheless, he went near to each one, near enough to hear. Then, when he had finished, he went up to the fish market, mostly deserted now, but with some people washing down the tables. He listened there, too, but it was the same. They were all speaking Catalan.

He tried the café, sitting at a table with Chantale, and slowly drinking coffee. This was the quiet time of the day for them and the waiters, now in their rough, casual jerseys, were just chatting.

At last he heard a voice which was plainly not Catalan. It belonged to an older woman, tired and thin, perhaps the wife of one of the fishermen about to go out, supplementing his earnings by a little casual work on her part. He waited for a chance when he could catch her on her own and then said quietly:

175

'I'm looking for Ramon's widow. Can you tell me where I can find her?'

She gave a little jump.

'Ramon?' she said.

'You know of him?'

'Ah, yes,' she said. Then she started to turn away. 'I cannot help you,' she said.

'It is for the family,' said Seymour.

'Are you police?'

'I'm from outside,' said Seymour. 'I'm English. Can't you hear?'

'Why do you want to know?'

'It is for the family, as I said.'

She still hesitated.

'Did you know Lockhart?'

'*Si*. I know of him. I know he gave her money.'

'Well, then.'

She looked around. 'They do not speak of Ramon around here.'

'Just the wife. A word. I mean no harm to her or to anybody here.'

'Very well, then.' She gave him an address. 'It's just up from the harbour. Next to the shop with the nets.'

A careworn woman opened the door.

'Señora Ramon?'

She looked at him apprehensively, but then was reassured when she saw Chantale.

'Can I have a word with you? It is not about Ramon but about another man. An Englishman. His name was Lockhart. I am English, too, and want to know about him.'

'He helped us,' she said. 'He gave us money.'

'Why?' said Seymour.

'Because he was like that. He helped many people.'

'Fishermen?'

'Yes.'

'And yet he helped you. Was not that a surprising thing to do? In view of what had passed? Was he not close to the fishermen?'

'He was, yes.'

'And had many dealings with them? Let us not say what the dealings were.'

'He had much to do with them, yes.'

'Was it not surprising, then, that he should go out of his way to help you?'

'Perhaps,' she said. 'But . . .'

'But what?'

'I think he felt sorry for us,' she said.

'About Ramon?'

'Yes.'

'He wasn't with the fishermen on this?'

'He felt they had gone too far. That it wasn't necessary. They could have just warned him off, couldn't they?' she said bitterly. 'It is not just the man who is punished but the family.'

'Would he have heeded the warning?'

She hesitated.

'He was stubborn,' she said. 'And we were desperate. He doesn't come from these parts. He's from Andalusia. They wouldn't have let him in, only I'm from here. From the harbour. My father was one of them. So they let him in, but they didn't like it. They felt I shouldn't have married someone from outside. And maybe they were right, for he didn't see things the way they did.'

'About the smuggling?'

'The smuggling was all right. It was what they smuggled.'

'Guns?'

She nodded. 'He said guns were a different thing. And why should he risk himself, and us, for them? It was not his cause, he said. Well, they didn't like it, but they would probably have let it go. But he was seen talking to someone known as a police agent. So they said, "He is going to betray us."'

'And was he going to?'

'We were desperate,' she said simply. 'They didn't let us have good places. We always had to fish where it was bad, and so he didn't catch much, and the children went hungry. And he became angry.'

'And then they killed him.'

'Yes. They are bitter men around here. I told him, and what they could do. "I am a bitter man, too," he said. "Poverty makes bitter men." But I knew what we were like.'

'I am sorry that they killed him,' said Seymour.

She shrugged.

'I think Lockhart was,' she said. 'And that was why he helped us.'

'He, too, was killed,' said Seymour.

'Yes.'

'I am trying to find out who killed him.'

'You won't find out,' she said. 'Any more than they will find out who killed Ramon.'

She looked at Chantale. 'And you, too, lady, had best be careful. You are not from these parts. And they do not like people who come from outside.'

'And yet they liked Lockhart,' said Seymour.

'He had money. And they were told he was on their side.' She shrugged. 'Well, I don't know about that. He liked the Catalans, it was said. But did he like all Catalans? Did he like people like them? He was angry about Ramon. They didn't like that.

'Well, now he is dead, too. Life is cheap on this coast. A fisherman's life is hard. It looks calm and sunny, and so it is during the day. But in the night a man can easily go overboard. The nets, you see, are heavy, and a sudden lurch can pull you. I know this because I have lived in this harbour all my life and so did my father before me, and his father. And both of them died early.'

* * *

'A farewell drink?' said Seymour, and led Ricardo into a bar.

'Farewell?'

Seymour nodded. 'I shall soon be leaving you. In a way, it is a pity, because I would like to see if Catalonia succeeds.'

'It certainly will,' said Ricardo confidently.

'It may, however, take some time,' said Seymour.

'We can wait.'

'I am afraid you may have to. Did not Tragic Week teach you this?'

'What I learned from Tragic Week was that next time we should have more guns.'

'Enough guns to fight an army?' Seymour shook his head. 'That is a lot of guns. Especially without Lockhart.'

'We didn't get that many guns from Lockhart.'

'Someone told me that his enthusiasm was falling off anyway.'

Ricardo looked at him quickly.

'That is not true,' he said.

'Isn't it? Someone told me he had been very unhappy about Ramon.'

'We were all unhappy about Ramon.'

'Lockhart felt, I gather, that it was unnecessary.'

'Some people argued that. I myself may have felt that. But those who were close to it were sure that he was going to tell everything. And you have to understand that for them it was not a game. Their livelihood depended on it. Their lives, even. Yes, they were devoted to the Catalan cause. But once they had got involved, it went deeper. They had put their families, their children, at risk. That's what I told him. It is not just a matter of romantic enthusiasm for a cause, I said. At some point it bites deeper. You have to be prepared to make sacrifices.

'Well, he flushed at that. "You don't think I'm serious?" he said. "No, it's not that," I said. "I think you are serious. But you're not serious like us." "Because I'm not Catalan?" he said. "You can't be," I said. "Don't think we're not

179

grateful. But in the end this is something we would kill for if we had to. And it's not like that for you. It can't be."

"I will show you," he said.

'Well, I didn't quite know what he meant by that. He would give us more money, perhaps? But I don't think that was what he had in mind. I think what he had in mind was what he did during Tragic Week. He went out on the streets and risked his life. Yes, I'm sure it was so that he could bear witness and perhaps stop some of the worst things from happening. That would be just the sort of Quixotic thing he would think of. But I think it was also to demonstrate that he was not afraid, that he was not some pussy-footing do-gooder, but was prepared to risk himself, like us. That he was, in a way, serious.

'And at first when I saw him out there I didn't mind. This will really bring home to him, I thought, what it's all about. He will see what we suffer and what they do to us. And then, maybe his feet will warm up. Because, yes, you're right, he was beginning to get cold feet. He wasn't so ready with his cash. "What are you going to do with the guns," he said, "when you get them? Kill more Ramones?" So, yes, he was beginning to get cold feet, and I thought that maybe what he saw during Tragic Week would stiffen his purpose. So I didn't mind, I didn't think he would be killed, of course. I didn't even think he would be put in prison. They don't usually put rich people in prison here, I thought they would have seen him and said, he's not doing any harm. Just another of those do-gooding, well-meaning nuts.

'Even when I heard that he had been put in prison, I didn't mind. That will bring it home to him, too, I said to myself. Because our prisons are not exactly holiday homes. He'll learn now, I thought, what the real world is like.

'And then, Christ, when I heard that he was dead, I couldn't believe it! Even him, I thought! Those bastards!

'So there you are, Señor Seymour. You've obviously been asking around and you've learned a few things. And maybe Ramon sticks in your gullet a bit, as it did in Lockhart's. But what you've got to realize is that this is Catalonia not England. You come from a country where life is easy. Well, it isn't here!'

'I came out here,' said Seymour, 'to find out who killed Lockhart. Not to take sides.'

'You *do* have to take sides,' said Ricardo. 'That is why he died.'

'Well, is it?' said Seymour.

'Is it?' said Ricardo, taken aback.

'Ever since I have been here,' said Seymour, 'people have been pushing me to take sides. That is the explanation, they said, the explanation for Lockhart's death, the explanation for everything. Catalans, Arabs, anarchists – even the Spanish. They all invited me to take sides and often that is an explanation. But I don't believe that it is.'

'You don't?' said Ricardo. He seemed stupefied.

'Let me put a case to you. Where your own arguments lead you, if you like. We know that Lockhart supported the Catalans. We know that he supplied money and contacts to enable them to buy guns – you, yourself, have told me this. Now we know, I think, that there was some kind of arrangement for them to be smuggled in by sea. Fishing boats would go out at night and pick them up from bigger boats lying offshore. We know that the Spanish authorities had got wind of this arrangement, and that Ramon was going to tell them more, perhaps all. And we know that Ramon was killed in order to stop that happening.

'We know also that Lockhart did not like that. He was angry. In fact, he was very angry. So what was he going to do about it? Because he was the sort of person, so several people have told me, who translated belief into action. When he believed something, he liked to do something about it. So what might he have been going to do about this?

'We know he had become lukewarm about the Catalan cause. He still, perhaps, believed in it and, as you say, he wanted to show you that he did, and so he went out into

181

the streets during Tragic Week. But that was to show you that he wasn't the man you were taking him for, just a – what was it you said? – a pussy-footing do-gooder. That, though, was a side issue. The real issue for him was what he was going to do about what he knew – that the Catalan fishermen had killed an innocent man.

'Well, of course, one of the things he might have done was to do a Ramon. Tell what he knew. And he had quite a bit to tell – about the arms and the sources of arms, about how they were transported, in what boats, and how they were brought ashore. And doesn't the same argument apply to Lockhart as it did to Ramon? If he told what he knew, wouldn't a lot of people suffer?'

'What are you saying?' said Ricardo, a thin spot of red appearing in his cheeks.

'Might not those who were involved have taken the same action with respect to Lockhart as they had done with respect to Ramon?'

'Killed him?'

'You said it.'

Ricardo rose from the table.

'I was a friend of Lockhart's,' he said. 'We were all his friends. He came to us and volunteered to help us. He did help us. I saw him out on the streets during Tragic Week. He was out there for us. Not just for us, maybe. But he was out there. When the bullets were flying. And if you think that any of us would have killed him, let me tell you, you are mistaken.'

As he turned away, Seymour said, 'Sit down. Of course, I don't believe that. I am putting it to you to show you where arguments can lead. If you start from one set of premises and not from another. Especially political premises. What I have found since I have been here is that people are very ready to offer you premises but less ready to consider other possibilities. And you, and the Catalans, are no different.'

* * *

182

As Chantale was approaching Las Ramblas, where she was to meet Seymour, a man on the other side of the street looked up and saw her, hesitated, and then came across to her. Chantale was surprised because she had thought she didn't know any men in Barcelona. She was even more surprised because this man was an Arab and decent Arab men didn't do this sort of thing. She began to feel alarmed. And then she recognized him. It was Hussein, Lockhart's office manager.

'Señora, forgive me – I did not intend to – but you were in my mind as I was walking along – that is,' he said hastily, embarrassed, 'Señor Lockhart was in my mind. He has been in my mind a lot lately. He was not just my employer, he was a friend, and when he died I lost more than an employer. I was very angry, and so were a lot of others. He had been a friend to us. That such a man should die like that! I was bitter against the Government. They shot us down and then they killed him.

'But since that time there has been much talk among us and I have come to think that things were not as I had supposed. I have been deliberating whether to speak to Señor Seymour about this; but then when I saw you coming along, I realized that it would be better to speak to you first.'

'First?'

'Of course, Señor Seymour must know. But first I wanted to know where the family stood.'

'The family?'

'Yes.'

'But why ask me?'

He stared at her. 'But, Señora, we have all presumed – you are a member of the family, are you not?'

'No,' said Chantale.

The manager seemed stunned. 'But, Señora, that cannot be! We have assumed – we have all assumed – it is not just me, Señora, it is everyone!'

'Look,' said Chantale, 'I have been aware, ever since I got here, of people looking at me strangely. And someone else has said – but I have met Leila and I do not see how I resemble her.'

'You wouldn't. She has grown older, of course, and she is anyway smaller than you. But, Señora, even I can see the resemblance! I did not know the young Leila, I was not here when she came, I was too young. But I know the family. I am myself a distant cousin. and I would have sworn –'

'I am *not*,' said Chantale, 'a member of the family.'

'Are you sure? What is your family name?'

'Fingari.'

'I think there are Fingaris somewhere in the family,' said the manager doubtfully. 'There could be. The family is spread all along the coast. Not just in Algeria.'

'What is the name of Leila's family?' demanded Chantale.

'Lungari.'

'Lun, Fin – I suppose it is possible. I shall have to ask my mother. But, Señor, I am only half Arab. My father was a Frenchman.'

'But you take, if I may say so, very much after your mother. And after – as I have said, it is as if the young Leila had walked into the room. That is what they all say, all the old people – but, Señora, if I have made a mistake –'

'You have made a mistake,' said Chantale.

'Then the family did not send you?'

'No,' said Chantale.

Hussein pounded himself on the head.

'I have made a dreadful mistake,' he said. 'But so have we all!'

'Why would the family have sent me?' asked Chantale.

'That – that, Señora, is what I wished to talk to Señor Seymour about.'

When Seymour appeared, they went with Hussein to his office. He seemed very perturbed and kept shaking his head as if he couldn't believe it. When they got to his office he stuck his head through the door into the inner quarters and spoke to someone and a little later they brought out a tray of cups of mint tea. Whatever the circumstances, hospitality had to be maintained.

He seemed to find it hard to begin.

'And so – and so,' he said at last, 'you are not a member of the family, Señora?'

'No,' said Chantale firmly. 'At least,' she added, 'I don't think so.'

'And they have not sent you?'

'No.'

The manager was silent. Then he said, 'In a way, that is a relief. You see, Señor Lockhart was much loved among us. He was seen as having put his life at risk during Tragic Week. For us. To see that we were not maltreated. To bear witness on our behalf. And when he died, there were calls for justice. There were calls that those who had killed him should pay the penalty.

'But nothing happened. No one was found. No one was brought to trial. And people began to murmur. And they said, "So this is Spanish justice!" and others said, "If we cannot have Spanish justice, then let us have our own." And then it began to be said that it wasn't as we supposed, and that he had been killed for quite another reason.

'In Algiers this would be seen as a family matter. And it was thought that it would be the same here. But then it was thought that perhaps his own family, since they were British, would not see the obligation. But if that was so, yet the other side of the family, Leila's side, certainly would. But nothing happened.

'So when you came, Señora, it was thought that the family had at last decided to take action. Many said that they should have sent a man, and others said, no, it was clever to send a woman, for no one would suspect a woman, and then when they met you, Señora, and saw that you were at home here, that you knew Spanish ways, it was said that

185

the family had been clever, that it had picked someone who would know their way around. And when you came, Señora, with Señor Seymour, they said, this is clever too. For he will help her to find the man who did it. So people saw there was a great family design.

'And there is another thing, too. For Leila has a brother, and he has been over here for some time. And for a long time people thought he would be the one to act for the family. But again nothing happened. So when people saw you, Señora, they thought that perhaps you had been sent to stiffen his purpose. That, perhaps, that was the design.

'Yet, lately, there have been other rumours. That the family is divided. That Leila herself is opposed. To the family taking its own justice. Those may be the ways in Algeria, she has said, but they are not the ways in Spain. And, since we are in Spain, we should do as they do. Leave it to the Spaniards to take justice!

'And I, myself, think that she is right. We are in Spain now and they have different ways. Besides, if she, the wife, says so, who are we to gainsay her?'

Chapter Thirteen

Looking down into the plaza they saw Nina sitting on the bench beneath the palm tree eating her lunchtime rolls.

They went down to her.

She looked up at them, with unfeigned pleasure in the case of Chantale, with indifference in Seymour's case. He wondered about this: was it an indication of a general inclination or was it just that she saw in Chantale a kind of mother, or perhaps an elder sister? But then he thought it was probably neither, just that she liked Chantale.

'May we?' he said, indicating the bench.

'Please do. I am waiting for my mother.'

Perhaps it was mother, then, thought Seymour, reverting to his previous thoughts.

'She'll be along in a minute.'

'Good,' said Seymour. 'I'd like to talk to her.'

She looked at him curiously.

'That's what you like to do, isn't it?' she said. 'Go round talking to people?'

'Well, I suppose –'

'Yes,' said Chantale, 'he does.'

'Actually,' said Seymour, 'the person I'd really like to talk to is you, Señorita.'

'Me?' said Nina, surprised. 'Haven't you talked to me already? Enough?'

'Not enough,' said Seymour. 'Señorita, I come to this late and from outside. And I do still not really have a picture of what actually went on here in Tragic Week.'

'It was terrible!' said Nina, shuddering.

'Soldiers?'

'Police at first.'

'Shooting?'

'Later. At first it was just shouting. Then it got to stone-throwing. Then the police charging with their truncheons. But then the men fighting back, with their fists at first, but then throwing things. They ripped tiles off the houses.'

'And where was Lockhart at this time?'

'He was out there, walking about.'

'Wasn't that a foolhardy thing to do?'

'Not at first. He stood a little to one side, so that he could see. And we knew why he was standing there like that, and everyone respected it. I think even the police respected it, for they let him stand there. There was a kind of –' Nina hesitated –'a kind of authority about him. I felt very proud of him.'

'And then the soldiers came?'

'Not at once. First it was the police, and then the police were driven off. There was a pause: and then the soldiers came.'

'Shooting?'

'Not at once, but very soon.'

'And your father?'

'Ran forward to protest. But his bodyguard held him back.'

'Yes, I heard that he had a bodyguard but I didn't really understand it.'

'They were Arab. I think they came from the Arab community around the docks. His manager, Hussein, had sent them. They suddenly appeared on the second day. He was surprised, I think, because he had not expected them. But after that they stood by him, even when the shooting started. They dragged him away into the houses. But then he insisted on coming out again, and they came with him. They stayed right through the day, and the night – the fighting went on through the night, this part of the town was in flames and you could see everything – and on into the next day. And then the soldiers charged, this time with bayonets, and our side got broken up, and I think it was at this point that the soldiers turned on him. I suppose they were excited and frightened and were turning on anybody. I didn't really see what happened at this point.'

'Because you had been injured?'

'Yes. I got knocked down, and somebody carried me away into one of the houses. And when I came to, I looked out of the window, and saw they were still fighting. But I couldn't see him, not any more. And someone said he'd been taken away, arrested!'

Seymour nodded.

'Right,' he said. 'I've got that. The general picture. Now here's another question and it's a particular question. At some point the Arabs joined in?'

'I don't think they were there at first. But after the soldiers had broken us up, they began to spread out through the houses. I don't know what they did, but when they got to the Arab quarter, the Arabs began fighting back. That was when it all got very bloody.'

'And Abou appeared at this point?'

'Abou?'

'Do you know him? Leila's brother.'

'I know him, yes.'

'Was he there?'

Nina thought. 'Yes, he was certainly there. But – but what he was doing I do not know. He didn't really join in the fighting. He was sort of creeping around. I think he was looking for my father. Perhaps Hussein had sent him to try and persuade my father to come away. I heard him say – I was still there then, it was just before I was knocked down – heard him say to them, the ones who were guarding him, "Where is he?" "It's all right," they said, "we're looking after him."'

'And Abou himself?'

'Was terrified. I don't think he knew what was happening. His eyes were staring and he was looking around. I thought he was half mad. But then, we were all half mad.'

'This was just before you were knocked out?'

'Yes. And when I came to, the square was empty, except for the bodies lying there, and I couldn't see my father anywhere. I rushed down and went out. People kept trying to stop me. I looked around for him but I couldn't see him. There were others looking for him, too. Do you know Manuel? He owns the café just around the corner. He was there, too, looking. I heard him ask for Lockhart. He was asking one of the bodyguard. But the man was wounded and dazed and didn't seem to know what was going on. He said that my father had been taken away by the soldiers. "Where has he been taken?" said Manuel. And someone else said, "Yes, where has he been taken?" I remember now. It was Leila's brother. "Yes, where has he been taken?" he said. "To the prison," said someone. "The prison!" said Abou. Yes, I remember now, it was Abou. "Are you sure?" And he struck his head with his hand. And then he rushed off. To tell Hussein, I think.'

'Thank you,' said Seymour.

When Nina's mother came, they sat talking on the bench for a while, until Nina had to go back into the school. They all got up together.

Nina's mother held out her hand to Seymour.

'I am afraid I am going back to Gibraltar tomorrow,' she said, 'so I may not see you again.'

'Oh, you may,' said Seymour. 'Since we shall be going over to Gibraltar tomorrow ourselves.'

'You are?' said Nina's mother. 'Perhaps you can come and visit me, then, that would be nice.'

'It would be very nice,' said Chantale, who had not known until now that she was going to Gibraltar.

'I remember you saying,' said Seymour, 'when we talked before – or perhaps I heard you talking to the Señora in the hotel? – that you had some calico to dispose of?'

'Yes,' said Nina's mother. 'She doesn't want it. Nor do I, really. What am I going to do with calico? You can't do anything with it, really. Not unless you're a boat!'

'Well,' said Seymour, 'I might be able to find a use for it. Perhaps we could pick it up from you when we call?'

'My God, he's back!' said a voice in the guardroom.

'He's come back especially to get you, Ferry!' said another younger voice which Seymour immediately recognized.

The midshipman came out.

'Hello, sir! Nice to see you back with us,' he said.

'It's nice to be back,' said Seymour.

'And your lady, too, sir?'

'In the offing,' said Seymour.

'Would she care to join us this evening, sir? And you? In the mess? That would give us all a lot of pleasure.'

'I'm sure it would. However, there is somewhere else I have to visit first. The stores.'

The midshipman swallowed.

'The stores. Right, sir.' He hesitated. 'This afternoon, perhaps, sir?'

'Now.'

The midshipman squared his shoulders.

'Right, sir. Now.' He raised his voice. 'Mr Ferry?'

'Sir?'

The petty officer came hurrying out of the guardroom.

'Mr Seymour would like to visit the stores. Now.'

'Now, sir?'

'Now.'

'Things are not quite as shipshape as we would wish, sir –'

'That's all right.'

'We could perhaps get things in better order by this afternoon –'

'Now, please.'

191

'Right, sir. Now.'

'Would you like me to accompany you, sir?' said the midshipman, loyal to his subordinates and hoping possibly to avert in some way –

'Perhaps I could join you later? In the bar. Oh, and is there any chance, do you think, that Admiral Comber might be there?'

'I think there's a very good chance, sir.'

Ferry led Seymour into the stores.

'What would you like to see, sir?' he said despondently.

'Nothing.'

'Nothing?'

'I just want a private word with you.'

'Private word? Yes, sir, of course, sir.' They went into a tiny boarded-off room.

'Sir?'

'Ferry,' said Seymour, 'how long have you been here?'

'Been here?'

'At Gibraltar.'

'Ten years, sir.'

'You will remember, then, the switch to oil?'

'Big thing for us, sir.'

'But difficult, I understand. Particularly at first. Before the big contract went through.'

'With Anglo-Persian? That made all the difference, sir. Before that we were really scraping around. "Those bas- tards –" begging you pardon, sir, but that's the way the Admiral used to talk, especially when he was referring to the Admiralty – "have got me down to two days' supplies. More efficient like that, they say. Just in time. That's the expression they use. But how am I supposed to fight a war on that basis?"

'"Christ, sir," I said, "we're not going to fight a war, are we?" "Maybe not," he said, "but I've got to be sure we're in a position to do so. What I need is some bloody oil!" "Why don't you try Mr Lockhart, sir?" I said. "He's got good contacts. He'll be able to find you some if anybody

192

can." "You think so, Ferry?" he said, going all thoughtful. "Dead certain, sir," I said. "He's got contacts all over the place. I know that because – well, I just know that, sir. I'm sure he'll be able to help you. Mind you, he might have to cut a few corners." "There are no corners on the sea, Ferry," he said, giving me a wink. "Don't you know that? At least, not as far as I am concerned."

'Well, maybe not as far as he was concerned. But there were as far as the Admiralty was concerned, and he got hauled over the coals. That was when he used the Language, sir. But he always had time for Mr Lockhart after that. Said he'd got him out of a hole. And the country, too. And that the bastards didn't deserve it. Begging your pardon, sir.'

'Why, hello, Seymour! You back? Got your lady with you?'

'She might be joining us a bit later.'

'Like a tot?'

'Christ, is that a tot?'

'Navy style, Navy style. Here's to you. And to your inquiries. How are you getting on?'

'Pretty well there now, sir. Just one or two small points to clear up. The irregular shipments of oil, for example.'

'Irregular –? Never heard of it!'

'Before the Anglo-Persian deal.'

'I'm quite sure I've never heard of it.'

'To Gibraltar. I'm not saying they weren't needed. And this, actually, does not need to be part of my inquiries, nor of my report.'

'It doesn't? Have another one?' He signalled to the barman. 'Another one for Mr Seymour, and me. And make them a reasonable size, Edwards. None of this thimble stuff!'

'I did, though, have a question,' said Seymour.

'You did?' said the Admiral warily.

'I can see you had to cut corners to get hold of oil. Before the Anglo-Persian deal. There was something dodgy about your arrangements with Lockhart. However, they got you the oil, and that was what counted. For you. But perhaps not for the Admiralty auditors?'

'Bastards!' said Admiral.

'Yes, I'm sure. They usually are. But it put you in a tight spot afterwards from which, fortunately, you escaped.'

'The devil looks after his own!' said the Admiral, grinning.

'I suspect that while the auditors found out some things, they did not find out everything.'

'That is possible,' acknowledged the Admiral.

'And did not that put you in rather a spot with respect to Lockhart?'

'How so?'

'Well, he could have revealed what he knew.'

'Why would he do that? He had been paid. Handsomely.'

'Ah, but hadn't he also, in the process, acquired – how shall I put it? – credit that he might, at some point in the future, draw on?'

'Well, naturally –'

'Let me put it a bit more sharply, hadn't he got a bit of a hold on you?'

'Let's stick to the word "credit", shall we?'

'Or we could say "favours". He had done you a favour. Might he not reasonably expect a favour back in return?'

'That would not seem unreasonable.'

'What was the favour that he asked?'

'Well . . .'

'I think I know, actually. Or can guess.'

'You probably can, damn you, Seymour!'

'But you tell me.'

'Well . . .'

The Admiral finished his glass and put it down on the bar.

'What he wanted was a touch of the Nelsons.'

'Touch of the Nelsons?'

'A blind eye. To certain shipments.'

'Of arms?'

The Admiral nodded. 'There's a sort of informal agree-ment among the Big Powers in this neck of the woods that one Power doesn't ship arms to territories of another Power.'

'And you breached it?'

'Not quite. We didn't do anything ourselves. But we knew it was going on. And I guessed he had a hand in it. I knew it was for those damned Catalans that he was always so keen on. More trouble than they're worth, in my opinion, though I've got a certain respect for them. But I owed him something, so when he came to me – I agreed to a judicious touch of the Nelsons. But, of course, that wasn't the end of it.'

'No?'

'Not when he got killed. Because, you see, I thought he might have been killed because of that. Because he'd got mixed up in it. And I didn't like that. I felt I still owed him. So when they did nothing about it, I said, Damned if I'm going to let them get away with this! So I called in you.'

'You think he died because of the Catalan connection?'

'Dead sure of it!'

'I'm not,' said Seymour.

'Talking of Nelsons,' said Seymour, as he turned to go, 'you'll remember that part of my duties was to invest-igate theft in the stores. If you wished to take action – and I think a *little* frightening might be in order – you could centre it on a matter of some calico. But I'll leave it to you, sir.'

'Back to Barcelona, then?' said the Admiral, as they went out of the door together.

'Just for a day or two. And then back to England.'

'I knew a girl in Barcelona once,' said the Admiral nostalgically. 'Her name was Dolores.'

'Lockhart?' said Leila. 'Well, he was always a man of sympathies.'

'Catalan sympathies?'

'Arab, too. That's what attracted me to him in the first place. Here is a man who understands us, I thought. And so he did. Up to a point. But lately I have been wondering whether he really understood us. These things go very deep, you know.'

'And did you mind his sympathies? For people other than the Arabs?'

'No. Not at first, at any rate. It was all part of him. His generosity, his enthusiasm for everything, his idealism. I loved that, and I loved him.'

'But you changed. You said, not at first. Not at first: but later?'

'Well, maybe I did change.'

'Why?'

She was silent for a little while, thinking.

'I don't know,' she said eventually. 'Perhaps one grows older. At least, I grew older. I am not sure about him.'

'He kept the sympathies, while you gradually abandoned them?'

'Not just that.' She hesitated. 'I found that in his case they were mixed with other things.'

'Women?'

'Well, yes,' she said. 'Too often and too much.'

'People have told me that you forgave him.'

'So I did. Up to a point. But something died in me.'

'Did you hate them? The others?'

'Hate them!' She looked startled. 'Well, I suppose I did. Disliked them, certainly. That unspeakable creature in Barcelona! And there were others.'

'Also in Barcelona?'

'Yes. There was one woman especially. She – she flaunted him. As a conquest. "Look, I've got him. He's mine, not yours." Of course, she didn't really do that. I never met her. But I heard of her, and it was as if she was doing that. Deliberately, to hurt me. And yes, I hated her. But she went the way of all the others, so I shrugged, and let it rest. In the end he always came back to me.'

'And your family?'

Again she looked startled, and this time there was something else: she suddenly became guarded.

'My family?'

'Back in Algeria. How did they feel about it?'

'They didn't know about it. Not for a long time. But when they did hear about it they didn't like it. It wasn't so much the dishonesty that they didn't like, it was the shame. They felt that the family had been dishonoured. Their pride was hurt.' She grimaced. 'We Arabs are a proud people. Like the Spanish, only worse.'

'And your brother?'

'Abou?'

She took her time about replying.

'Well, Abou,' she said then, softly.

She paused. 'Well, Abou is a simple creature. He sees things in black and white. And the family is important to him.'

'So he came to you. But when he got to you, he found that you had changed?'

'Yes, I had changed,' said Leila, looking down at her hands.

'So he didn't know what to do?'

'What to do?'

'He came here to do something, didn't he? Or was sent to do something.'

Again she looked at her hands. 'It all seemed so simple to him. So clear. I had been dishonoured. The family had been dishonoured. It could not be let rest. But I reasoned with him. I said that things were not like that here. This was Spain and they did things differently. And if I was prepared to let it rest, so should he be. Well, of course, he couldn't understand that. And why should he pay any attention to what I thought? Women don't usually have much of a voice in my country. And the family had already decided. But, in his way, he loved me. And I think I could have persuaded him.'

'But then came Tragic Week.'

'Then came Tragic Week.'

'Abou,' said Seymour. 'I want to talk to you about Aisha.'

'Aisha?' said Abou, surprised. 'Farraj's daughter?'

'That's right. You knew her, didn't you?'

'I knew the family. At one time. Farraj worked closely with us.'

'Us? Your family? Or Lockhart?'

'Both. My family had had connections with Farraj's for a long time. In Algeria. And then when Lockhart became part of our family he and Farraj began to work closely together. They were almost partners. Farraj handled things for him in Algeria and Morocco, and then Farraj moved to Gibraltar to work even more closely with him.'

'And Aisha?'

'I got to know Aisha when Farraj came back to Algiers on visits, which he did regularly. Of course, I didn't take much notice of her at first. She was a girl. Just another of Farraj's family. But then on one visit I did.'

'You noticed that she had grown up?'

'Yes. She *made* me notice her. She spoke up. That is unusual in Arab families and Farraj was quite upset about it. It quite put me off her. I thought it was unseemly. But Leila said that was because she had lived in Spain and that was the way women behaved in Spain. And I grew quite to like it.'

Abou became embarrassed.

'At one point I even thought of marrying her. Leila would have liked that. She encouraged me. "What you need is a good wife, Abou," she said, "and Aisha would make you one." I even went so far as to ask her. Farraj first, of course, and he was not unwilling. But then when it was put to her, she refused. I could not understand that. She said that it was nothing personal but that she wanted her freedom. Farraj was angry with her. It made things difficult for a time and he left her behind when next he visited.'

'But you did not forget her?'

'No.'

'And you knew that she remembered Lockhart?'

'She was fond of him. She thought of him as another father.'

'And so it was easy to pressure her, when you went over to Spain yourself, to do something for him when he was in prison?'

Abou gave him a startled look.

'That wasn't part of the original plan, was it? It couldn't be, because you didn't know that he would be in prison. In fact, when you learned that Lockhart had been taken to prison, you must have thought for a moment that that had put a stop to what you intended to do. What you had been sent to do.'

'I don't know what you mean,' muttered Abou.

'But even before that, it seemed that Tragic Week had made what you planned impossible. But then you realized that it could actually work for you. Help you. With all the general chaos no one would notice or care. You went out on to the streets to find him. But then things went wrong. You suddenly discovered that he had a bodyguard. You couldn't get to him. And then you learned that he had been arrested and taken to prison, where you couldn't reach him. You had to think again; and you thought of Aisha.'

Abou did not say anything.

'You thought of a way of reaching him even though he was in prison. You would poison him in his cell. You made inquiries and found that food could be got in to the prisoners. But that meant talking one of the warders into it, and you thought that could be done better by someone other than you. And then you had an inspiration. You thought of Aisha. You got her to talk to the warder. And to persuade him to pass in some food which you had prepared. Poisoned food.'

'No, no. It was not as you suppose. How – how do you know this?'

'She was seen, Abou. Seen in Barcelona, and seen near the prison. And she told someone that she was arranging for something to be taken in to Lockhart.'

'She will not confirm this! You will not be able to talk to her. You will not be able to ask her that!'

'Why not, Abou? Why cannot she be asked in Algiers as well as she could have been asked here? And when she is asked, she will tell. Why shouldn't she? She has done nothing wrong. You tricked her, Abou, nastily, and she will not like that. She looked on Lockhart as a father, remember. And I do not think she will be cowed into silence, Abou, not this time. Her father sent her back to Algiers so that she should not be asked, and she went along with that as a dutiful daughter and because she was not quite sure herself what she had done, unwittingly, or how she had been involved. She was young and puzzled and confused. But she loved Lockhart and she is a spirited girl, Abou, and now she will not be silenced. She will tell all right.'

'How will you reach her to ask the questions? She is married and her husband's permission will have to be obtained. And she is in Algeria! And my family –'

'Your family, yes. In which family feeling is so strong. So strong that it could not bear the shame and disgrace of what Lockhart had done to Leila. So strong that it sent you, Abou, as Leila's brother, to take revenge.'

'I will speak to Farraj! And I will speak to my family. They will not allow –'

'It does not matter what they allow or do not allow. You are in Spain now, not Algeria. And it will be by Spanish law that things will be decided.

'And as to reaching Aisha, I am not sure that you will find Farraj as much on your side as you think. And if he is not, nor will his friend, her husband, be. Aisha will be allowed to talk. And she will have plenty to say. And, besides – besides,' said Seymour, 'I, too, have family in North Africa.'

And that, too, he suddenly realized, had now become definite.

Chapter Fourteen

'But – but he was a good chap!' said Hattersley, bewildered. 'I always got on very well with him.'

As if that was a sufficient guarantee of his innocence.

'Well, there you are!' said Seymour.

'I must say, it comes as a surprise. I was sure all along that it was the Government. Or the Catalans. Or the anarchists. Or the Arabs.'

'Well, it wouldn't have been the Government, would it? I mean, why wait to get him in jail before killing him? When there were so many better opportunities during Tragic Week. I must say I agree with you about the Catalans, though. For a long time I thought they had a hand in it.'

'You did?'

'Oh, yes. But why should they kill the goose that was, from their point of view, laying the golden eggs? At one time I toyed with the idea that some of them might have thought he was going to betray them. There was a fisherman, you know, that was probably going to do that, and they killed him. But Lockhart? Who was out on the streets during Tragic Week trying to act as a safeguard for them? It didn't make sense.

'As for the anarchists, there obviously is a lot of anarchist activity in Spain and the police and the prison governor all assured me that it was the work of anarchists. But about the only anarchist I could find with whom Lockhart came in contact was his daughter, Nina. And she was a very isolated person. If there was an anarchist cell, she was about the only one in it.

'Then there was the rumour about the wife of the high-up. Well, there was such a person and I talked to her. Like so many others, she had an affair with Lockhart. But, like so many others, it didn't last. In the end, as you told me, he was always true to Leila. I thought maybe it was a case of jealousy. But she was a very high-handed lady and, although she might stoop to murder, she certainly wasn't prepared to stoop to employing an Arab to do it.

'That brought me back to the Arabs. And that brought me back to Lockhart's wife, and her family, who were the Arabs that Lockhart was most in contact with. And here there was certainly motivation. Lockhart was betraying his wife all the time. She certainly resented it. Could she have been the one who set the killing in motion? Well, she could, but Leila herself was a complex person who had grown, and wished now to put a lot of things behind her, many of those things which she had brought from Algeria.

'But, remember, although she had discarded them, others hadn't. In particular, others in her family. Many in the family were still bound by tradition and in particular traditions of honour and dishonour and revenge. Try as she could, she couldn't escape from these traditions. Even though she was now in another country. They sent over Abou, her brother, a man who knew only these traditions. An honourable man, in his way, who loved his sister and couldn't bear to see her slighted and, as he saw it, dishonoured. She worked on him, however, and might have succeeded, but ran out of time.

'So there you are. The difficult thing for me was to distance myself from everyone's suggestions. Everybody thought they knew the answer and was eager to give it me. Before they had asked the questions.'

Of course, strictly speaking, Abou, and the prosecution of the charges against him, did not fall within the preserve of the Chief of Police, since Abou was in Gibraltar, and that, according to the British (but not the Spanish) was not Spain. For a few days it looked as if Abou might slip down the crack between them but the crime had definitely been committed in Spain and the Foreign Office, stiffened by the Admiral, was prepared to concede the practical, although not theoretical, point. By some legerdemain, the details of which remained obscure but which somehow involved a boat, the surprised Abou found himself in Barcelona, when he passed into the hands of the ever resourceful Chief of Police.

Not resourceful enough to satisfy his wife, however.

'As a Chief of Police, Alonzo, you are a disgrace. It's time you did something about it. Otherwise, we're going to have to spend the rest of our lives in this dump, whereas, as I've made clear to you from the first day of our marriage, my mind has always been set on Madrid. That's where I've always seen myself. I think I would feel at home there. But all through our married years I have seen the prospect of that dwindling over the horizon.

'It's time you pulled yourself together, Alonzo, and now you've got the chance. Mr Seymour has given it to you. He has solved the mystery of who killed Lockhart and given the solution back to you. Now all you've got to do is claim the credit for it. Oh, and now that you've got the murderer safely in prison, keep him there! Do you think you can do that?'

'Of course, I can, Constanza!' said the Chief reproachfully. 'He's in safe hands.'

'Well, he wasn't last time,' said Constanza. 'At least, Lockhart wasn't. You let someone creep in and poison him. It could happen again. I might even do it myself. That bastard killed Lockhart and someone ought to get him. He extinguished the one light in my life.'

'You say these things, Constanza, but –'

'And I mean them. He was the only man, of many, that I've ever really cared about.'

The Chief felt compelled to tackle Constanza.

'Constanza,' he said, 'there have been rumours about you.'

'Only silly men listen to silly rumours,' she said.

'Nevertheless –' he began.

'Of course I slept with Lockhart,' she said impatiently. 'And very enjoyable it was, too. Unlike with you, Alonzo!'

'Constanza –'

'*And* with half of the male population of Barcelona,' she said.

'I know you don't mean this, Constanza –'

'And if I have any trouble with you, Alonzo, I shall sleep with the other half. And while we are on the subject, Alonzo, you've been drinking far too much lately. It has made your performance suffer. And I am not talking about your performance as Chief of Police. Cut out the drinking, Alonzo, and I, too, might be prepared to practise abstinence. Up to a point. Particularly if I saw a chance of getting to Madrid.'

Nina, despite reservations about the Spanish legal system, was pleased that the murderer of her father had got his deserts. Lockhart's death, however, meant the end of his financing of the anarchist school, since Leila was not in the least interested in anarchism and disliked Nina, a sentiment reciprocated by Nina, who wouldn't have accepted the money if it came from Leila anyway. The school closed, as anarchist schools usually do: but then, again as usually happens with anarchist schools, another took its place.

This one was Nina's own and had a special character. This one was located in the Arab quarter and seemed to everyone, Arabs, Catalans and Spanish alike, about as Quixotic a venture, and as foolhardy, as any of those espoused by her father. It seemed, however, just the sort of thing you could expect from the Lockharts and, to everyone's surprise, succeeded. Moderately. Nina had envisaged a school which would bring Spaniards and Arabs and Catalans together. That, many felt, was not very likely.

The Arabs near the docks, however, gave Nina their support, possibly, as Ibrahim claimed, out of traditional Arab sympathy for the afflicted, but possibly out of residual loyalty to Lockhart. After a while a few Catalans, mostly from the fishing community, appeared, muttering darkly. And then a few Spaniards, usually of an anarchist tendency. The Chief of Police kept a fatherly eye on it; on the school, that is, and not, as Constanza regularly claimed, on Nina. And, surprisingly, the school prospered, or at least, lasted. Indeed, when, after some time, the authorities threatened to close it, Catalans, Arabs and Spaniards united in its defence, so perhaps Nina achieved her aim after all.

The *cabezudos* were as usual cavorting around on Las Ramblas, and, as usual, as soon as they saw Chantale they made a bee-line for her.

They formed a circle around her. Chantale stood her ground.

'Come and scratch my back, pretty lady!' one of them pleaded.

'When he says back, pretty lady, he means somewhere else!' said another *cabezudo*.

'No such luck!' said Chantale firmly.

'A ride? On my back?'

'When he says on his back, he means on your back, pretty lady!'

'No chance of that, either,' said Chantale.

'Will it be done soon, pretty lady?'

'Will what be done?'

'What you have come from Morocco to do.'

'That is not something you should ask me,' said Chantale. 'You should ask my friend.'

The *cabezudos* broke up and took up a new formation.

'We're squaring the circle,' they said.

'So I see,' said Chantale.

'Are you going to square the circle, too?'

'Which one?' said Chantale.

'The one that began with Lockhart.'

'A circle finishes where it starts,' observed another *cabezudo*.

'With Lockhart?' said Chantale.

'Who else?'

'But if you are going to square the circle, you will have to do it soon,' said the first *cabezudo*.

'Before next week,' said the second *cabezudo*. 'Because otherwise you'll have to go out to Algeria to do it.'

'For the first time since I have known you,' said Seymour, 'you are behind the times. The circle has already been squared.'

The *cabezudos* cantered away and then stopped and conferred. Then they came back.

'Congratulations!' they said, and bowed.

'And now we are in another circle,' said Chantale. 'It is an old circle and a private one.'

'And are you going to square it?'

Chantale looked at Seymour, and Seymour looked at Chantale.

'We think so.'

'Ah!'

The *cabezudos* danced away and then came back.

'Congratulations!' they said.